DARK WATER UNDER THE BRIDGE

DARK WATER UNDER THE BRIDGE

BRIDGE

PARKS PAT MYSTERIES #3

P.D. WORKMAN

ISBN: 9781774680735 (IS Hardcover)

ISBN: 9781774680728 (IS Paperback)

ISBN: 9781774680742 (IS Large Print)

ISBN: 9781774680698 (KDP Paperback)

ISBN: 9781774680704 (Kindle)

ISBN: 9781774680711 (ePub)

pdworkman

ALSO BY P.D. WORKMAN

AND MORE AT PDWORKMAN.COM

That all fears may
be overcome

STYLE NOTE

Since my largest readership is in the USA, I have chosen to use US spellings throughout this series. That includes the Americanization of centre to center, even where it is an actual place name, just for consistency's sake. I apologize to my Canadian readers for this.

I have chosen, however, to use Canadian grammar, particularly for Canadian voices. If you see what you think is a grammar error, it may just be Canadian, eh?

CHAPTER ONE

The sun was still low in the sky, orange light filtering into the kitchen. Margie "Detective Pat" Patenaude was sipping her morning coffee and staring into the depths of her fridge, trying to decide whether to make herself a bag lunch to take to the police station with her, or whether she would take a break and go find something over lunch. She hadn't explored many restaurants near the office, so she wasn't sure what was available. Not that she was that picky.

"The same things are in there as the last time you opened the door," Christina teased, echoing the same words Margie used when her daughter stood staring vacantly into the fridge. "Nothing new is going to materialize while you stand there with the door open."

"You're a smart aleck," Margie told her.

But Christina was right. Margie already knew what was in the fridge, and inspiration wasn't going to strike just because she was standing there with the door open, letting all of the cold air spill to the floor and raising the energy bill. She sighed and closed it.

"I don't know what I want today."

"We need to go shopping. Get something good."

"I think you're right," Margie agreed. They could go to the

Co-op, or the No Frills down Seventeenth Avenue, and stock up on some easy to prepare meals. Margie never seemed to have the time or energy to make much when she got home from work.

The phone rang. Margie looked at it, hoping it would just be some telemarketer so she could ignore it. She didn't want to have to deal with a real phone call so soon. She didn't even have one cup of coffee down yet. But it was Detective Cruz, a Filipino-born cop on her team.

"Patenaude," she answered briskly.

"Is this Detective 'Parks' Pat?" There was a note of amusement in Cruz's voice.

"Parks Pat?" That was a new one. Margie understood where the nickname came from, of course. Since she had moved to Calgary, she had been primary on a murder in Fish Creek Park first, and then a similar one in Glenbow Ranch Provincial Park. They had not been related, except by circumstances, but both had been reported in the news, and it would seem that she had now earned her homicide team nickname. Parks Pat.

"That's what they're calling you," Cruz acknowledged.

"Well, okay. It could be worse. What did you need?"

"Have you ever been to Ralph Klein Park?"

Margie let out a puff of breath. "Ralph Klein Park. No, I haven't even heard about that one. Is it out there near Glenbow?"

"No, actually this one is close to you. That's why I figured you might have been there. It's new. Just opened in 2011."

Margie thought about the little park she had visited while taking Stella out on a walk with Christina. It had a little pond and a splash park for young children. She couldn't remember the name off the top of her head, but was sure it wasn't the one that Cruz was talking about. "Another provincial park?"

"City of Calgary park, this one. Though it might be out of city limits, I'm not clear on that. It's right on the eastern edge of the city, anyway. Think you could get out there?"

"Yes, of course. What... am I going to find there?"

"We've got another body. Sorry."

Well, that was to be expected when she worked homicide. "Another body in another park? But we know it isn't either of the same killers, because we already caught them both. They're locked up where they can't do any more harm. Was it the same cause of death?"

"You'll have to get more information when you get out there, but preliminary indications are that it is not. No visible stab wounds on this one."

"Good. I think if it was the same cause, I might have been a little freaked out."

"We're all a little on edge. I'm going to head out there before long too; I'll back you up."

Margie wondered why he hadn't gone to investigate first. If he was the one who had taken the call. "I'm primary on this one? Why?"

He chuckled. "Because they asked for you in particular."

"Me?"

"Parks Pat. They figured if it's in a park, you should be the one in charge."

"That's just—"

"I know. And don't worry, I'm sure that sooner or later you'll get a body that wasn't found in a park. But for now, that's your assignment. Go to the park, make nice, find out what you can about our newest victim."

CHAPTER TWO

Christina assured Margie that she would be ready to get on the bus when it arrived and wouldn't be late for school. She was grown up enough to deal with her own transportation. And Margie knew the fifteen-year-old could handle it. She had been going to the high school via bus since the first day, when the body at Fish Creek Park had been discovered. Margie had promised to drive her that day, but it had not worked out. As a teenager, Christina was as independent as Margie would let her be. Margie figured she should be thankful that she wasn't getting constant requests to be driven here and there all over the city. Calgary sprawled over a huge area, and it could be challenging to get from one end to the other. So far, Christina had been content just riding the bus between the house and the school.

So Margie left Christina to finish getting ready and climbed into her car. She put the park's name into the GPS. She quickly braided her long black hair and coiled it into a bun and waited for the GPS to start receiving coordinates from the satellite and plotting a course. She should be happy that she was being assigned to parks. She enjoyed being outside, connecting with nature. She liked to walk and hike and might even take Stella out there with her one day. For sure she was going to take the whole family out to Glenbow Ranch. When she was off and could arrange it around Christina's school schedule. She would schedule a golf cart tour so that they could take Moushoom, Margie's grandfather, with them. He would like it there. Sometimes, the Nakoda out that direction participated in ceremonies in the park. Moushoom would really love that. They didn't speak the same language or come from exactly the same culture, but Moushoom would understand the symbols and the ceremonies.

The GPS beeped and the robotic voice directed Margie what direction to drive. She put all other considerations aside and focused on following the GPS instructions. Despite her Métis heritage, she had a terrible sense of direction and, if she made a wrong turn, it could take another twenty minutes to get back on track again. Not just because it was sometimes difficult to get turned around if you ended up going the wrong way on a highway or main thoroughfare, but also because she was totally capable of then getting back on the exact same road headed the wrong direction a second time. Or getting flustered and taking another wrong turn.

So she kept an eye on the GPS screen previewing the curves and intersections ahead so that she would not miss any exits or turn the wrong direction. She was glad that Cruz had mentioned it was on the edge of or just outside the city, or she might have started to panic when she ended up driving alongside golden brown fields in an area that felt too remote to bother with a park. But she remembered how Glenbow Park was down in the valley below the highway so, even with its vast size, it had been invisible until she had driven down the last road.

There were a couple of signs, and then she could see a few people walking or cycling to the left of the highway. She turned onto the access road into a grouping of trees. The road curved toward a building that looked like it was built with children's blocks. The medical examiner's van and the forensic team were there, pulled up onto the sidewalk. Rather than parking beside them, Margie followed the road past the building to a public parking lot. It probably filled up on a weekend, but early in the morning on a weekday, it was quiet. A few scattered vehicles. Unlike at the provincial parks, there were no Conservation Officers in gray shirts waiting to drive her in an electric golf cart to the scene of the crime. She had seen a small group of people gathered past the playground, so she knew where the body was and it wasn't too far to walk.

Margie got out and strode towards the big education center. She walked through a small plot of short apple trees that declared itself The Orchard. The apples were turning from green to a rusty red. Some were scattered on the ground with two or three small bites out of them. Not the work of squirrels, by the size of the bite marks.

She stopped when she got to a railing and looked down. What Cruz had not bothered to mention to her was that Ralph Klein Park was a wetland. She stared down at water, which was nearly black and seemed bottomless. The education center jutted out over the water, walkways around it in two tiers up above the water. She swallowed and looked around to focus her mind somewhere else.

She circled the education center around the land side. There was an unusual playground like a pile of sticks, a zip line stretching away from it toward a pond or canal where the rest of the crime scene investigators were. Margie picked up her pace and strode toward them.

Bodies in the water could be ugly. Bloated up with gases, swollen and unrecognizable features, skin starting to separate from the flesh. Predator and insect activity.

But she would stay calm and keep things moving forwards. She would be strong and professional and there would be no issues.

One of the figures by the water waved at her. Margie nodded and joined them just outside the yellow tape perimeter. The group parted so that she could see the woman's body. She was wearing a white blouse and dark blue or black pants. She was face-down in the water, close enough to the shore that they would be able to pull her out without hip waders.

"You're Detective Pat?" a man in a Calgary Police Services uniform and black mask asked.

"Detective Margie Patenaude, yes," she agreed. "Who discovered the body?"

"Early morning jogger. Over there." He nodded to a young man in tights and a jacket sitting some distance away from the scene. "I've got a brief outline from him, but you can take his statement."

"And this is where she was? He didn't move her?"

"He says he didn't touch her."

"Okay, good. Do you think he did?"

The constable considered her question seriously. She took the moment of silence to read his name bar. Archambault. "I don't think he did. It's natural to reach out to someone like this, check to make sure they're really dead and that it's not just a mannequin. But his shoes were relatively dry." Archambault looked down at his own shoes. His shoes and pant cuffs were covered in mud.

Margie raised her brows. "So, you did touch her?"

"Just did what I'm supposed to. Made sure she was good and dead, then came back here and called your team. Preserved the scene."

There was a large area cordoned off with yellow tape. Margie would have made it bigger, but it was a judgment call.

"You checked for a pulse?"

"Just radial. It was obvious touching her that she was dead."

"Rigor?"

"Yes. And… sodden. She's been in there a few hours."

Margie didn't feel the need to touch the body herself to verify this. She felt sorry for Constable Archambault. But she'd had enough opportunities to check for life signs herself. It was one of the less enjoyable parts of being a law enforcement officer.

"Thank you." She nodded to him.

He nodded back his thanks. Margie looked at the body again.

A sweeping glance. She was trying not to commit more to long-term memory than she could help. "Did she have a purse? Wallet? Anything to identify her? There's no missing person report?"

Everyone there shook their heads. Margie looked around. "Let's protect any nearby garbage cans or bins. Extend the perimeter up and down the stream another... twenty-five meters. Watch for footprints. She didn't fly into that water. Someone killed her here or dumped her here. We want to find out all that we can about that. Surveillance video in the parking lot?"

"We're waiting for someone from the education center to get here. Apparently, they will have access to the security video," one of the forensic guys advised.

"Okay." Margie hoped that there was good video. They wouldn't have been able to identify the killer in the Fish Creek case if they hadn't had good video footage. Multiple pathways, several cameras in the parking lot, and even wildlife cams had enabled them to establish the people who had been in and out of the area the victim was killed in. That made it a lot more practicable to find the killer.

"I'll let you guys work out the best way to get her out of the water and collect any evidence," she told the forensic team and the doctor from the medical examiner's office, whose nametag identified him as Adrian Galt.

They seemed to be happy that she wasn't telling them how to do their job. Margie was sure they would be much better at working out the best procedure than she would. And she wouldn't have to get any closer to the water herself.

CHAPTER THREE

*I*t was a while before someone from the education center came out and met Margie a short distance from where the forensic team was erecting screens. Margie was afraid it would be a teacher or docent who didn't have any authority or in-depth knowledge of the park, but the tall, thin man who introduced himself as Arby Finkle seemed to be in charge of operations there. He wore a suit and tie, which seemed excessively formal.

He was literally wringing his hands, his expression deeply distressed. Margie was glad Finkle couldn't see the body past the screens. He might have had a complete breakdown.

"I'll need you to tell me everything you can about the security here and..." Margie tried to focus, "about the water system. Some of this is man-made." She motioned to the deep pool she had first seen adjacent to the parking lot. "I just need as much background as you can give me. Whether or not you think it would be relevant."

"Of course, of course." Finkle wrung his hands more. He looked at her with great intensity, eyes glittering with emotion. Becoming aware of his hand-wringing, he tried to hold still, but he just ended up squeezing the blood out of both hands until they were as white as the woman's corpse. "I can't believe that something like this could happen here. Why would anyone…" He shook his head, not even able to finish the sentence. Margie waited, hoping to hear whether he said 'kill someone here' or 'dump someone here.' Which did he think it was?

But he didn't finish; he just shook his head, sobbing in a low thrum Margie could barely hear.

"We will need the security video," she prompted, trying to get him started.

"Yes. Of course. I'll get you whatever I can."

"Whatever you can? Don't you have a fully operating system?"

"Well… yes, most of it is functional. What we have."

"I don't like the sound of that," Margie warned.

"Yes… well, we've had some vandalism over time, and it takes the city time to get around to fixing it. Our little park isn't exactly high on their priorities list. There are probably buildings downtown they are more interested in. City Hall. The new library. You know, they'll get *their* security fixed a lot faster than us."

"How long has it been out of service?"

"Well… a while," he admitted, unwilling to put a time estimate on it.

"Get me what you can." However much that was. She was gathering from his reluctance that there wasn't going to be very much at all. Would they at least have something showing who had been in the parking lot during the hours before the woman's body was found?

"I am sorry," Finkle apologized. "There is more coverage inside the education center. We have some very valuable displays, so we want to keep them protected…"

"Yeah. That makes sense," Margie said flatly. Not because she was feeling gracious. She could see that they had not prioritized the security of the park itself. The indoor footage was not likely to help them much unless the woman and her killer had been in the education center before she had been killed, which Margie thought was unlikely.

She pulled out her phone and thumbed through the photos,

including the ones that Dr. Galt had texted to her just a few minutes earlier. The victim was wearing a semiformal blouse and slacks, not a t-shirt or other casual wear. She suspected it might be the uniform worn by the education center staff. The ones who didn't dress quite as formally as Finkle.

"I'd like you to see if you can identify the victim for me," she said slowly. "Do you think you're up to looking at a picture?"

"Yes, of course."

Margie didn't show it to him. "You need to be prepared. I am going to show you a picture of the dead woman's face."

He nodded impatiently. The two hands with the death grip on each other stayed intertwined, and he leaned forward, waiting for Margie to show him the picture.

"You need to understand what the water does to bodies," Margie warned. "There hasn't been a lot of animal or insect predation yet, but her face will seem quite swollen. It may be difficult to recognize her."

"I want to help in any way I can."

Margie waited for a few seconds longer, then finally turned the phone around to show it to Finkle. He stared at it without expression for a long few seconds. Margie expected him to shake his head and tell her that no, he didn't have a clue who it was.

Finkle turned away from her and, for a moment, Margie thought he was going to unlock one of the doors to the education center and take her inside. But that wasn't why he was turning away from her.

He staggered a couple of feet away and threw up. Margie took a couple of small, discreet steps back. It was a few minutes before Finkle regained control of himself. He wiped his mouth on his sleeve and turned back to her, looking miserable.

"I don't know who that is."

"Okay. Thank you for giving it a try." Margie hesitated. "Why don't you go on in, get yourself together and have a glass of water or cup of coffee and, when you're ready for me, let me know." She handed him one of her business cards. "Just give me a quick call or shoot me a text when you're ready."

"I'm sorry…"

Margie waved the apology away. "No. It's a shock, and you weren't prepared to see that. You're certainly not the first guy to react that way."

"It's not like it is on TV, or seeing a picture in the paper."

"No, it's not."

He nodded and wiped his mouth again. "I'll just be a few minutes, then," he said, and walked away from her, heading for the education center.

❧

MARGIE DIDN'T NEED to supervise the technicians as they gathered their evidence for Dr. Galt as he prepared the body for transport. She was the most senior law enforcement officer on the scene, but they had much more training than she did in handling evidence and they knew what they were doing. After the medical examiner's van drove away, Margie stood watching the forensic team searching through the garbage cans. The whole process included taking pictures of the garbage cans before they were touched and laying everything out on a plastic sheet. Harvesting one layer of trash from the can at a time as if it were an archaeological dig. They needed to be able to say exactly which layer anything suspicious had come from.

Detective Cruz arrived. Margie gave him a brief update. They stayed outside the yellow tape at the bank of the creek and around the garbage cans. As far as Margie knew, they hadn't found any footprints that would be helpful.

Of course not. That would have been too easy.

"No ID yet?" Cruz asked.

"No. Hopefully, they'll find her wallet or purse in one of the garbages, or drag this part of the stream to see if it was dumped here with her."

Cruz looked up and down the waterway at the area that had been taped off, and seemed satisfied with it.

"What have you found out about the water system?" he asked. "Was she killed here? Dumped here? Or was she dumped somewhere else and the water carried her downstream?"

Margie breathed shallowly.

"I assume she was just dumped here. The water doesn't seem to have much of a current. I guess we'll hear more from the medical examiner. I'm waiting for this guy," she motioned to the education center, "to pull himself together so he can answer some questions about how she got there, what else we need to know about all of this... water."

Looking upstream, she saw a floating dock, where several children sat examining the contents of buckets of water scooped out of the stream. Her stomach turned over queasily.

Cruz looked at her, then at the children. "What's wrong? You think they're going to dip something out of the water that's evidence in the case? The woman's wallet or fingers or something?"

"She still had her fingers," Margie protested.

"Well, the way you were looking at them..."

"I just... I'm worried about them being out there. It doesn't look safe."

Cruz looked at them again.

Margie tried to keep her tone casual. "They're kneeling on the edge. The adults are several meters away. If one of the kids went in..."

"It would probably scare them. But as you say, there isn't any noticeable current. And there is a lifesaver right there that their dad could throw to them and one of those rescue hooks to pull them in."

"Oh, is there?" Margie pretended that made it okay. "I didn't see that. Right."

He gave her a quizzical look but didn't pursue it. "So... what's with the monument on top of the hill? Is that some kind of memorial?"

"I didn't go to the top yet, but I guess it's some kind of art installation. There are actually three monoliths and some berms. I'm afraid it's a bit highbrow for me. I don't really *get* it."

"Doubt if there's anything to get. I'm not much of a modern art guy myself." Cruz looked at the garbage can the forensic techs were currently going through, and the screens still up at the water's edge. "Tell you what, why don't we go up for a look?"

Margie agreed. She didn't want to get in the way of the investigation. They wouldn't think much of her if she ended up messing with any of the evidence.

She and Cruz walked down a gravel path along the river, then up the small hill to gaze at the art installation. Tall grasses and wildflowers grew beside the trail.

"Well... I still don't get it," Cruz admitted, staring up at the monoliths.

"Me neither."

They looked down at the crime scene. Margie realized that from their elevated position, she could see over the screens. They should have used a tent. At least it had still been early morning and there hadn't been a bunch of kids or their mothers at the top of the hill, hysterical because they had seen the dead, drowned body of a woman on the other side of the screens.

CHAPTER FOUR

hoops," Margie murmured, looking at the screens. There was nothing to see anymore, so it was too late to do anything about it. But the next time, she would remember to look up at possible vantage points.

Cruz chuckled through his mask. "Glad we didn't end up in trouble over that. Let's go down to the dock."

The 'we' was generous, since Margie had been the one in charge of the scene and Cruz hadn't even been there when the screens were set up. Margie walked down the hill with him, and then along the path to where the children were dipping minnows out of the stream into their buckets. Cruz stepped confidently from the land onto the gray plastic cells that formed the little dock. Margie stayed back on the path. Cruz walked up to the edge where the children were and started a conversation with them. The father stood close to Margie, a tall, sandy-haired man. He looked at Margie.

"You're police?"

"Yes. Detective Patenaude. My partner there is Detective Cruz."

"What's going on here?"

Margie knew he would find out eventually anyway. And he wasn't likely to be calling any reporters.

"There's been a death."

"A murder?" he asked immediately.

"That hasn't yet been determined."

The man looked toward the screens. "I don't think too many people just come out here and die of natural causes. It isn't like it's a swimming hole or the ocean."

Margie shrugged and didn't agree or disagree. "How long ago did you and the kids get here?"

"Oh, about twenty minutes ago. We're homeschoolers," he explained, "this is a really good hands-on activity. They like the education center, but the best part is getting out here and playing in the water."

"Sounds like fun." Margie smiled, but she didn't go out on the dock. She let Cruz talk to the children. He seemed to be enjoying himself. Her queasiness returned when he leaned out over the edge to look into the dark water. "So you didn't see anything unusual when you arrived today? Anything that seems different or out of place?"

"Just you guys. Normally it's pretty quiet this early in the morning. A few people out getting exercise. Walking, running, biking. Sometimes we see other homeschoolers out here, but most families don't get out until later in the day."

Margie looked around, her eyes sharp for anything in the area that didn't belong or might have been dropped by the killer. It was pretty clean, no garbage blowing around. But the water was murky. She couldn't see down into it. It was impossible to tell how deep it might be out at the edge of the dock where the children were or what might be under the water.

"Are they safe over there? Should they be wearing life jackets?"

"No, they're here all the time," he told her with a tolerant smile. One of those parents who thought she was overprotective and nothing bad would ever happen to his kids. But he hadn't seen the things that she had. "They know what they're doing, and I'm here if anything happens. Which it won't."

But before she and Cruz had approached, he'd been looking down at his phone. Reading his email? A text from his wife? Facebook? His eyes had not been on the children, even though he should have been showing more caution than usual with his awareness of the police presence.

"You haven't had anything unusual happen around here the last few days? People around who you don't know and who don't look like they belong? Arguments? Smells or sounds that were out of place?"

"No." His brows came down in a frown. "You don't mean that a dead body has been here for a few days, do you? I would think that someone would have noticed that."

"We're still in the very preliminary stages of investigation. We can't make any assumptions."

"Well… no, I haven't seen anything unusual. It's just been normal."

"Thanks. Can I get your contact information in case I think of something else I need to ask you?"

He was hesitant. "I said I don't know anything. I don't know why you would need to ask me any other questions."

"You never know when I might need the insights of someone familiar with the park. You can't beat the knowledge and insights of someone who has boots on the ground." Margie laid it on as thickly as she dared.

The man looked pleased. "Yes, of course. I guess that makes sense. And we really know our way around here. If you have any questions about the wetlands, my kids probably know more than the teachers in the education center, they've been here so much."

CHAPTER FIVE

*M*argie waited until Cruz was finished talking to the children, and looked toward the education center to let him know that she wanted to go there next. He walked back over the dock, making the floats bounce up and down in the water as he moved over it. The kids laughed in delight.

"Find anything out from the dad?" he asked once they were a distance away.

"No. Got his information just in case, but I don't think he knows anything helpful. How about the kids?"

"Good kids. Really into the wetlands thing. They could tell you all kinds of things about how these different features filter stormwater naturally. But anything about how a body got in the creek? No."

"As long as it's not their mom."

"I think someone might have mentioned if they were missing her." Cruz agreed dryly.

"I want to see if the head guy here, Finkle, is ready to talk to us yet. He was a little bit... wobbly after seeing a picture of the dead woman."

"Yes, I can see how he might be. You thought it was a good idea to show it to him?"

"I thought it might be someone who worked here. Went out for lunch and never came back... something like that."

"And did he know her?"

"Didn't recognize her. But drowning victims bloat up so much..."

He nodded. "Still could have been an employee."

"Hopefully, he's settled down enough to talk now. I want to get security video from him, and any information he can provide on how things work around here. Whether she was dumped there or washed down from somewhere else..." Margie trailed off. She started walking around the building.

Cruz held out his hand to stop her. "We don't have to go all the way around the far side of the building. We can get to the front doors from this side. Just over the catwalks. They go all the way around."

Margie looked at the catwalks over the deep, dark water. "I think I'd rather go around the other way."

"This is more convenient, and we've already seen the other side. Come on." Cruz strode toward the nearest walkway. He paused to look back after a minute. "Come on, Patenaude. You afraid of heights?"

"No."

"Let's go, then."

Margie looked for a reasonable excuse. She wanted to check on the techs out by the creek again. She thought they might have missed a garbage can in the corner of the building. She wanted to check under the unusual playground equipment to make sure nothing had been dumped there. But they would all have sounded like fake excuses. Which they were.

She dragged her feet after Cruz. He made it look so easy. He was very casual as he stepped from the gravel path to a small grill-work bridge. To Margie, it was nearly as bad as the pictures she had seen of the glass lookout over the Grand Canyon. Why couldn't it at least have been concrete? Why did it have to be something with holes in it?

She forced herself to walk over the bridge and followed him onto one of the boardwalks that hugged the building. They weren't actually boards, but were fully concrete and shouldn't have been a problem for her like the grillwork. However, the railing along the side was an open mesh or grill that she could see through to the still, dark, bottomless water. She grasped the top rail, and it was all she could do to keep from gripping it like a drowning man. She just steadied herself, tried to keep vertigo from kicking in and making her stumble or fall. It was like her worst nightmare, the thought of falling into the dark water in the pool beneath her.

Cruz looked back a couple of times, but kept going, not stopping to help or harass her. They climbed a metal flight of stairs to go up to the second level. Farther from the water, but a longer distance to fall if she went over the edge. She didn't know if it was better or worse. Finally, Margie managed to make it around the walkway to the building's front entrance where Cruz was waiting. He raised his brows. Margie couldn't see his mouth under the mask, but it didn't look like he was laughing at her.

"You *are* afraid of heights."

"No." She looked down at the black glassy surface. "Water."

"You're afraid of water?"

Margie tried to shrug it off. "Everyone is afraid of something. That just happens to be mine."

"You were really struggling to get over there."

"Yes." She waited for him to laugh and tease her about it.

"Good for you. You kept going and you did it."

Margie stared at him, surprised at the response. She hadn't expected any kind of understanding. He was a tough cop. And he came from the Philippines. An island. Surrounded by water. He had probably been in the water every day of his life before immigrating to Canada. It was as natural for him as breathing.

"I have kids," Cruz said, turning toward the doors and pressing a call button. "My youngest, Alejandro, he has anxiety. He's afraid of a lot of things. The doctor says that the only way for him to get over the fears is to push through them. Willingly expose himself to them and push through. Like climbing a hill." He gestured at the hill with the monoliths on top of it. "Eventually, the anxiety peaks, and your body will start to relax and recover."

"Yeah. That's what they say. Avoidance just makes it worse. But avoidance sounds much more attractive."

His eyes crinkled at the corners. "I'm sure it does. But you were brave and went ahead and did it anyway. And you survived."

Margie smiled back at him, her face warm. "Thank you."

The door opened and Finkle stood there. He seemed a little better than he had been when Margie saw him last. A bit more color in his cheeks. He still wrung his hands, though it was less obvious.

"Detective Pat. And…" He looked at Cruz. "Detective…?"

"This is Detective Cruz. He's helping me out today. We've taken a look around, and I wonder if you're up to answering some questions now."

He nodded and escorted them into the building. He took them to a lobby where there was some seating. They all sat down in a close grouping.

"Are you feeling a bit better?" Margie asked Finkle.

"Yes, a bit, thank you."

"Have you had a chance to pull your security footage yet?"

"I'm working on it."

She wondered whether they were ever going to see any footage. When he said that a lot of the cameras didn't work, what did that mean? Did it mean there was *no* outdoor footage? Or nothing beyond a view or two in the parking lot? And if so, how many people knew that? Had the killer known that none of his movements would be recorded?

"I told Detective Cruz that you were not able to identify the individual in the picture I showed you," Margie said. "I wonder, though, whether it might have been an employee that you don't know well, or that the water might have distorted her features enough that you just didn't recognize her."

He looked nervous. Probably afraid that she would make him look at it again to make sure that he couldn't identify the victim.

"She was a young woman," Margie said. "Mid to late twenties or early thirties. Blond, shoulder-length hair. No obvious scars, tattoos, or distinguishing features."

He considered this. "There are a few employees who could meet that description."

"Do you think you could give me their names and maybe call to make sure they are okay? You can say that there was a computer problem and you wanted to check when their next shift was. You don't need to say it's anything to do with the murdered woman or our investigation. We would just like to know that all of your employees are accounted for. The ones who could meet that description."

"Uh… okay." Finkle nodded. "I can do that." He looked at them for a minute uncertainly. "Right now?"

"You said there were just a few employees who meet that description. It wouldn't take long to check in with each one, would it?"

"No. I guess not. I thought you would have other questions, though. Then I'll call once we're done."

"Okay. Have you had anything strange happen in the last week or two? It doesn't need to be anything violent. Just whether there were any unusual occurrences. Arguments. Flower deliveries. Phone hang-ups."

"No, I can't think of anything. The education center was closed until school started again, so it's only been a couple of weeks. Everything… has seemed pretty normal. I mean, as normal as anything during the pandemic. It's a bit different with masks, social distancing, and sanitizing anything that the kids might touch during a tour. It's more work. But we're doing everything we can to keep the students safe."

"Of course. Have any of the employees taken unexpected vacations? Called in sick? Just not been available when you thought they would be?"

"No."

"Anyone sick at all?"

"Of course we've had a few people sick. But not the virus. Everyone was tested."

"No, I didn't mean that. It's more about whether everything has just been routine or there have been unusual scheduling changes."

"I can't think of anything. When you work with young people, there are always some changes. They decide they have to go away with friends for the weekend, and if you say no, then they call in sick at the last minute." He rolled his eyes. "And you know very well that they aren't really sick, they just wanted to make it to that party or wedding."

Margie nodded. "*Millennials,*" she offered.

"Exactly. It isn't the way we were raised, I'll tell you. The work ethic just isn't the same."

"And you didn't have anyone do that the last couple of weeks? Since you reopened after the summer?"

"No, I don't think so. We haven't been back for long enough."

"And everyone has been working together well? Nothing unexpected? No personality changes since you were last operational?"

"Personality changes." His brows came down like he didn't like her choice of words.

"Sometimes, when people are stressed about something or have had big changes in their lives, it shows up as changes in personality or behavior. Someone very patient before is suddenly blowing their top unexpectedly. A sloppy employee suddenly seems OCD or vice versa. Someone is jumpy. Has unusual fears." She didn't look at Cruz as she said this.

Water was not an unusual fear. Well, maybe it wasn't common, but people did drown. It was dangerous, even for people who didn't think it was.

Finkle thought about this. His hands slowly stopped their wringing motions, and he smoothed his fingernails with the pad of his thumb. "Well… there was Patty."

Margie nodded, waiting. She pulled her notebook out and worked the pencil free of the coil where she had stashed it.

"She seemed overly emotional. I thought... maybe she was pregnant. Or she could just have PMS. I don't know. It isn't like you can ask a young woman these things. She just seemed like that. Hormonal."

"What is Patty's physical description?"

"She's... medium height and build. Thirty or so."

"Blond?"

"Yes, I suppose so. Light brown or dark blond."

"Do you have her number?"

He shifted uncomfortably. "In my office."

"You don't have it on your cell phone? Employees never call when you are away from the office, or you don't need to phone them to line up substitutes if someone calls you after hours to say they can't make it the next morning?"

Finkle hesitated. Margie was beginning to get impatient with him. She wasn't sure why he didn't want to call any of his employees, but he needed to get with the program. They needed to identify the woman out in the water. Patty? Another employee? Someone not associated with the park at all?

"Mr. Finkle. I want her number. Give it to me now, or go to your office and get it. Now."

He started to flush red. Not angry. A lot of men would have been furious to be spoken to like that by a woman. Or a cop. But Finkle wasn't the aggressive type. He was embarrassed or scared. He ducked his head, reminding her of a turkey.

Finkle pulled his phone out of his pocket. An older model, small screen, not one of the modern oversize ones. He tinkered with it for a moment, presumably finding the contacts app and then filtering down to Patty's name and checking her contact information.

"Do you want me to call her? Or do you want to?"

At this point, she was worried that he would completely screw it up if she let him make the call. For whatever reason, he didn't want to call his employee in front of Margie. Were they having an affair? Had he made up the part about her being moody or hormonal?

"Just give me the number, please."

He read it out to her. Margie wrote it down. "Okay. Give me a minute." She got up from her seat and walked away from Cruz and Finkle, turning her back on them. She walked far enough away that it would be difficult, if not impossible, for Finkle to hear what she was saying in a normal tone of voice. She dialed the number into her keypad and took a deep breath, unsure what she would say if Patty answered the phone. Apologize and say it was a wrong number? Explain that she was with the police and just doing a welfare check? Say that something had happened at work and she didn't want Patty to come in without knowing that there was something wrong?

The first three rings went unanswered. Most people, if they were going to answer, would do so within three rings. But sometimes the phone was across the house, or they were already on a call with someone else, or the phone started ringing on Margie's end before a connection was made. She had no idea what the cell coverage was like at the education center. She pulled the phone away from her ear for a moment to check the bars. Weak, but still connected. She put it back to her ear and waited. The tone continued to ring, and ring, and ring.

Patty wasn't there. Or she wasn't someone who answered unidentified phone numbers. Plenty of people screened by the Caller ID and wouldn't chance talking to a stranger. Especially Millennials.

Eventually, the call clicked through to voicemail. Patty hadn't recorded a message of her own, but let the default automated message answer. Margie hung up. She could try again later when they had identified the victim. Or when they hadn't.

She walked back to Finkle and Cruz. "No answer. Does she usually answer her phone?"

Finkle thought about it. He nodded slowly, hesitantly. "Yes. I think she was pretty good about it. It's hard to remember, you know."

"Yes. I'm sure you have a lot of people to keep track of. Can you give me the names and numbers of the other women who might answer the general description I gave you? Patty and who else?"

He worked through a few names, spelling them out for her and digging their numbers out of his phone.

CHAPTER SIX

hen they left Finkle, Margie tried Patty's number once more. She looked at Cruz while she waited for an answer she didn't expect to come.

"What did you think of Finkle?"

"Nervous guy."

"Definitely. Very anxious."

"But… at the same time, not the type I would expect to be involved in a homicide. I don't think he's anxious because he did something. Just because he's a naturally anxious type and doesn't know how to react to a police investigation."

Margie nodded. She hadn't picked up on a lot of deception flags from him. A few, but not a lot. More hesitant and unsure of how he was supposed to act than lying or being evasive.

The call went through to voicemail again. This time, Margie left a message. Very generic, giving her name and asking Patty to call her back. No mention of police or an investigation. It could be anything from a telemarketer to a bank manager or a school-teacher wanting more information about booking a class program. She hung up.

They were walking in the direction of the forensic techs to see if they had found anything or needed any additional assistance or direction. Which Margie was sure they didn't need. Instead, she called Detective Jones, who she hoped would be at her desk with the computer in front of her.

Kaitlyn Jones answered, her tone cheerful but not too bouncy. "Detective Pat?"

"Hi, I wonder if you can check for me and see whether there is a missing person report filed on Patty Roscoe."

"Sure, hold one minute."

They continued to walk as Jones looked it up. She was back a couple of minutes later. "Yes. Entered just this morning."

Margie looked at Cruz. "Bingo."

"You think this is our victim?" Jones asked.

"I think it is. She's an employee at the education center out here who might have been under some additional stress lately. Fits the description of the deceased. We couldn't reach her on the phone; I took a chance it might be her."

"I'll follow up on this end. Get as much information as I can."

"Get whatever pictures you can, any background, criminal history, social networks. Who reported Patty missing?"

"Husband."

"He just reported it this morning?"

"Yes."

"Where was he last night?"

There was silence from Jones as, Margie assumed, she read through the highlights of the report that had been filed. "He figured he couldn't report it until she'd been gone for twenty-four hours. Then he decided he couldn't wait that long and made a call."

"Hmm." Margie knew that many people still thought that they had to wait twenty-four or forty-eight hours before they could report someone missing. But they usually started the process early anyway. Or started making calls to hospitals and were told by them to make a police report. "Okay. Well, start gathering what you can. Have someone bring the husband in for an interview. We'll get there as soon as we can."

"Will do," Jones agreed.

Margie hung up. She looked at Cruz. "How long would you take before you started making calls about your missing wife?"

He considered. "I'd probably be calling the last place she was supposed to be once she was an hour late. Then calling her friends, colleagues, anyone who might have known what her plans were. By the time it was a couple of hours, I'd be pretty worried. Of course, my wife doesn't go out a lot. If she was someone who was routinely unreachable for hours at a time, or who had a history of disappearing for a night here and there, then I might not call until the next day."

Margie made a mental note of these details. It was always good to see it from someone else's perspective. There were people that you would start worrying about if they were twenty minutes late for an appointment, and there were people you wouldn't start *really* worrying about for a day or two. It depended on the person. But the way that Finkle had talked about Patty, he had made it seem as if she was a usually dependable employee who had only started having problems recently.

They reached the tape perimeter, and Margie and Cruz stood outside of it, waiting for the opportunity to talk to someone. The tech who seemed to be in charge, Mitchell, according to his name badge, drifted over to them. He had a clear face shield, so Margie wasn't concerned when he lowered his mask to speak with them.

"How is it coming, detectives?"

"We've probably done about as much as we can here. How are things going with you?"

"Going to be a while yet. Calls in to see how long it would take to get equipment here to pump out some of this water and drag for any larger foreign objects. May not be feasible, but we'll see."

Margie indicated the hill with the monoliths on it and pointed out about the screens not being enough to keep prying eyes from the body, if it had still been there when visitors had started to arrive on the site. Mitchell looked up at the hill, chewing on his lower lip, and nodded.

"Hadn't even thought about that. But it was early. They got her out of here before there was a lot of foot traffic."

"That's not always the case, though. I'm just as much to blame; I never thought to look up there and see what the sightlines were."

"Next time, we'll both be wiser."

Margie nodded. "Yeah. We may have a name. It probably won't make any difference to your work, because you're not going to throw anything away that has another name on it, but our victim may be Patty Roscoe."

"Patty. Okay." He did a rapid mental review of whatever they had found thus far. "I don't think I've seen that name or any P initials on anything we've pulled today."

Margie's surprise must have shown.

"You'd be surprised at how much stuff gets thrown out in these garbages. School assignments, employee shift schedules, coffee cups and lunches with names or initials on them. But I don't think we got any Pattys."

CHAPTER SEVEN

*O*ne of the tragedies of murdered or missing cases was that the people who were closest to the victims, those who ended up reporting their friend's absence or death, were the people who were most suspect in any violence against them. Spouses and significant others, parents, children, best friends. They all worried about their loved ones, called the police to try to get some help, and ended up under the microscope themselves.

So while Margie always went into an interview with the knowledge that they might be talking to a murderer, she also kept in mind that they might be completely innocent, genuinely grieving the loss of a loved one. And, of course, many people were both the culprit and the chief mourner. They weren't exclusive.

At the police station, Scott Warner had been welcomed, given a bottle of cold water, and settled into an interview room pending Margie's return. She looked in on him before entering the room. He looked around the room restlessly, not distracted by his phone, and also not crying or banging the table, insisting that someone deal with his missing persons report. There was no outrage over being left alone in the room while they looked into his report. No obviously guilty behavior.

"I'm just going to freshen up for a minute," Margie said. "Then we'll see what he has to say."

She took a quick washroom break, splashed water on her face, and chugged a mug of coffee before re-masking and entering the room to speak with her suspect.

"Mr. Warner. I'm sorry for keeping you waiting. We have been investigating. My name is Detective Patenaude. May I…?" She gestured to the chair opposite him as if she needed his permission to sit down. Put him in a position of power. Make him feel like he had control over the interview.

"Yes, please. Have you found anything out? I called the hospitals, but they won't say anything over the phone. And I worried about what if she was brought in unconscious or had amnesia, how would they even know who she was then? Have you checked?"

"If she was taken to the hospital, she would have had her ID, wouldn't she?" Margie countered. "They would be able to figure out who she was."

He looked confused for a moment, then nodded. "Yes. Right. Of course. They would know. But they wouldn't necessarily talk to me. More and more patient rights these days, they won't tell you anything without the patient's permission, and if she is unconscious and can't give it, then what?"

"We haven't heard anything back from the hospitals yet. You'll have to wait a bit longer."

Warner sighed and nodded. He looked down at his phone, thumbing it on, looking at it, waiting for it to ring. Maybe Patty would call him to tell him her car had broken down. Or that she'd been hit on the head, but was okay. Something that would mean she wasn't gone from him forever.

"Why don't you tell me about your wife?" Margie said. "I know you've already made an official report. Filling out all of those routine questions. But that doesn't give me a real taste for the person that she is. There is so much more to a person than just the physical description and what their last movements were."

Warner nodded. "Yeah. That's so true. Patty is… a wife and mother first and foremost. We have two young children…"

"Was she a stay-at-home mom?" Margie asked, already knowing the answer was negative.

"No. But not because she didn't want to be. If we'd been able to afford it, then of course we would have. But they have a good daycare, and Patty is really good at her job. She loves teaching at the education center. She was thrilled to be able to put her degree to good use. She was passionate about the environment."

"She sounds like a really special woman. Tell me about her movements? When did you see her last?"

"When she went to work yesterday morning. I picked up the kids from the daycare after I got off work, like I usually do. She gets home after me… then we have supper, put the girls to bed…"

"But you became concerned when…"

"She didn't get back from work when she normally would. I called her cell phone a few times, but she wasn't answering. I know she doesn't answer if she has a class or tour, or if she is in a meeting with her boss. But when it got to be a couple of hours… well, she's never done that before. She's always at home, never more than an hour late. And even if she was running a few minutes late, she would have called to let me know that she was late, and when she expected to be home. She was very good about that. Better than me." His voice cracked a little.

And he was the one who was supposed to be picking up the kids. Margie didn't imagine it went over very well if he were running late and forgot to inform either the daycare or Patty.

"No calls at all? Had you talked to her during the workday?"

"Yes. Once or twice. I don't remember specifics. You know, we just check in with each other now and then. Ask the other person how it's going or call to vent about our jobs." He rolled his eyes. "Even if you love your job, there are still those days when nothing goes right."

"Of course. So, you don't know what times you talked to her?"

Margie nodded to Warner's phone. "You can check your call log…?"

"Oh… I would have called her from my work phone. Not this one."

Margie let that sit for a minute before going on. "Okay. So maybe a couple of times during the day. Have you called anyone at her work? To ask what time they saw her last or when she left?"

"No. I don't know her coworkers. I know first names, of course; she talks about different people she is teaching with, or who she likes or doesn't like. In a superficial way. She didn't hate anyone, of course. Some people would just rub her the wrong way, get on her nerves."

"How about her boss?"

"Uh…" He looked blank. "I really can't tell you. I know her supervisor… that's… Sally something. And of course, the director, that guy." Warner shook his head, blinking and trying to recall. "Fink? Barney?"

"Arby Finkle."

"Yes. Him."

"Did they get along? Or did she have problems with him?"

"I think they got along okay. I know that she and some of the other workers… well, they made fun of him a little. Behind his back, not to his face." He shrugged. "Not mean-spirited or anything. Just like you do at an office. Blow off some steam talking about the stupid things your boss does."

"Sure," Margie agreed in a neutral tone.

"I guess he was kind of… I don't know. Fussy. Maybe a little…" He gave a limp-wrist gesture. "You know."

Margie looked at him, head cocked to the side slightly. "What?"

"I don't think that he was, but they talked about him a bit. About maybe he was… closet gay. Like… *Tinkerbell-Finklebell.*" Again he tried to shrug it off. "Just all in fun. Not serious."

"I see." Margie didn't write anything in her notebook, but continued to look at him, waiting for more.

"I don't know. She got along with everybody okay. And she liked the job. It was important to her."

"You weren't able to contact anyone from her work. So what did you think had happened? Did you think that she was still at work, or that something had happened to her on the way home? Or just that she was out running errands and might have stopped in to see friends?"

"I thought... maybe an accident on the way home. That's why I was calling hospitals." He rubbed at the corners of his eyes. Margie couldn't see any tears, but that didn't mean that there weren't any threatening. Or that he wasn't grieving just as much as the spouses who came in weeping like fountains.

Margie nodded. "She wouldn't normally have been anywhere else between work and home? Stopping at the grocery store? Gas station? Did she ever go out with friends for a drink or coffee?"

"No. She came home. We did errands at other times. She would come home to help with the kids. Making dinner and putting them to bed."

"Who made dinner?"

He looked at her like she was crazy. "What?"

"Did you make dinner or did she?"

"Yesterday?" he asked blankly.

The night before, he had obviously been the one to make the evening meal, if he were telling them the truth.

"Normally. Did you alternate? Did you make it because she got home later than you? Did you agree on certain days?"

"Well, no, Patty was usually the one who made dinner. I was so tired at the end of the day, you know, and I brought them home from daycare, so when she came home from work, it was her turn. I just wanted to relax in front of the TV for a while."

Margie nodded. "So she usually made dinner arrangements. Or maybe if she knew she was running late, she would tell you to go ahead or would pick something up on the way home?"

He shrugged. "Yeah. Maybe."

"So, you had to make the dinner instead last night."

He nodded.

"How did that make you feel?"

His eyes widened. "How did it make me feel?" He demanded, his voice startlingly loud. "I was sick with worry! I made the kids some KD and gave them a cookie when they were done, but I couldn't eat a bite. I was just... I could barely function. I didn't know what to do. Who to call. I was alone there, just the kids and me, and I didn't know what to do."

"That must have been difficult."

"It was! You have no idea what it's like just to have someone... not come home one day."

Margie nodded slowly and made a few notes in her notebook. "We would like to talk to the kids. Where are they?"

"They're... I took them to daycare. I didn't want them around here. I knew I would be waiting around and they would be bored. And I don't want them... wondering what's going on."

"What do they think happened to their mother?"

"They don't know."

"I mean, what did you tell them? What explanation did you give them?"

"I just told them that she would be home later. They wanted her to get home, but they didn't really ask about what she was doing. Just when she was coming home."

"And when did you tell them she was coming home?"

"Soon. I didn't want to say anything specific."

"We would still like to talk to them. How old are they?"

"Two and four." He shook his head, scowling behind his mask. "They're too young to be able to tell you anything. All they know is that Mommy didn't come home last night. You talking to them... it's just going to traumatize them."

"We'll be very careful. I'll have Detective Cruz help out. He has young children at home."

In truth, Margie didn't know how old Cruz's children were. But she imagined they were young. Either way, he was a dad. He was understanding of his son's anxiety rather than being impatient and macho about it. He was clearly good with kids. He would treat Warner's children kindly.

"No." Warner shook his head. "I don't give you permission to talk to my kids. I don't have to, right? You can't talk to them without my permission."

"It depends on the circumstances." Margie made a note in her notepad. "We'll do what we can without them, but I'd like to be able to discuss this with them too."

"They're too young. They don't know anything, and you'll just confuse and upset them. I've heard of how police can plant false memories." He stared at her accusingly, as if she had already told his children that it was his fault their mother was missing. "I don't want anything like that to happen."

"I understand that. Of course we'll be very careful not to traumatize them or to plant any suggestions—"

"No. I already told you no. No way. There's no way you're talking to my kids."

His expression was fierce. Margie remembered the home-schooling dad at the park and how casual he had been about protecting his kids near the water. On the other hand, this father was not taking any chances on exposing his children to something that might be harmful to them.

She nodded and went on. "You've given a description of your wife's car in your report?"

"Yes, of course."

"Have you had any car trouble lately, anything that might make you more concerned about a traffic accident? Or maybe a stall beside the road, leaving her stranded?"

"Just the usual. You know how it is with cars. Something always needs to be fixed."

"How was your wife's mental state lately?"

"I don't know…" He thought about it. "Okay, I guess? I mean, everyone has stress in their lives…"

"She hadn't had any unusual stresses lately? Any signs of depression? Drug or alcohol use?"

"Why? What does that have to do with anything?"

"Is it possible that your wife could have harmed herself?"

"No. I don't think so." His answer was certain at first, then less so. He stared off into the distance, thinking about it. "She had her down days, like anyone else. But she wasn't *always* down. She didn't talk about killing herself."

"Not everyone does. Has she been moody lately? More impatient? Wanting to be by herself?"

"Maybe."

"Do you have contact information for some of her friends? Her family? People who she might have talked to? Maybe even a doctor."

"She was estranged from her family. Doctors... I don't think she even has a GP. She just uses a walk-in clinic if she needs to get something checked out for herself. She has a pediatrician for the girls, but it's so hard to get a good family doctor these days..."

"Friends? She must have had someone she talked to."

"I'll see if I can get into her computer. I honestly don't even know last names, let alone phone numbers."

"You didn't do anything with them? Double dates or group things?"

"Sometimes, but Patty was always the one calling them. I'd call a couple of my friends if she wanted a bigger group, but she was the... social director in the family."

"Don't try to get onto her computer. Bring it in here. Along with any other devices she might have. Tablets, cameras, sports watch, anything that will help us to build a picture of where she was going and what she was doing. Do not try to get onto them. Leave that to us."

He was reluctant, but nodded his agreement. "Okay."

"You don't know what kind of security measures she might have. Some of these devices will wipe if you enter the wrong information too many times."

"She wasn't that security conscious. Her password is probably one of the girls' names,"

"If you could write down their names, birthdates, any important birthdays or anniversaries, her parents' and siblings' names, your phone numbers, anything like that." Margie pushed a pad of paper and a pen across the table to him. They would probably be able to access her various accounts by subpoenaing them from the service providers, but she was interested in seeing what he would write down. How much did he know? Was he the kind of person who kept track of important dates and bits of information or not? She already suspected not. Patty was the one who had managed their social lives; he didn't even bother to know the names of her friends.

She watched him puzzle over the information.

"Was Patty having problems with anyone? Any arguments? Threats? Phone hang-ups?" she asked.

"No, I don't think so. Not that she mentioned."

"You say she was estranged from her family. Why is that?"

"She…" he looked for a way to answer the question politely. "They didn't approve of all of her choices."

Margie considered. The woman's body had not had any tattoos, significant scars, or multiple piercings. Patty had married and had two children. She had a good education and was working in a good, respectable position that utilized her strengths. Any parent she could think of would have been delighted with her choices. She was not a free-spirited rebel.

"Does that mean they didn't like you?" she asked baldly.

Warner turned white. He looked at her and tried to decide how big his lie would be.

"They didn't, did they?" Margie pressed. "For whatever reason, they took a dislike to you. We're going to talk to them. And that's what they're going to say. So you may as well be truthful about it. Lying will only make it look worse."

"Okay, yes. You're right. They didn't approve of me and of her marrying me. They didn't think I had much going for me. But I've always been devoted to her and the girls. I've always worked to help support the family. I'm not some kind of deadbeat."

"Sometimes, people just rub each other the wrong way. Maybe they liked the guy she dated before you, so they were disappointed that she dumped him. People are emotional creatures more than logical."

He nodded along with her, the tension around his eyes relaxing. "I wish there was something I could do to make them like me better. But they don't, and Patty didn't want to do anything with them because of it. So we never really had a chance to make it up."

He twisted the wedding ring on his finger.

And it was too late now, whether he knew that or not.

CHAPTER EIGHT

$\mathcal{M}$argie met with the rest of the team after she was finished her interrogation with Warner. They did not tell him that they knew Patty was dead. She hadn't been properly identified yet. She might not be who they thought. Once they had confirmation that it was her, and had everything they could get willingly through Warner, they would let him know and see how he responded. She suspected that he knew she was dead already. Even if he hadn't had anything to do with her death, he knew when she didn't come home that night. She had either walked out on him and the children or something bad had happened to her.

"It sounds like there might have been some issues at work," Cruz suggested, leaning forward on the conference room table. "He can say all he likes that making fun of Finkle and telling stories on him behind his back is good fun, but the fact is, Finkle probably knew about it. A guy like that might not look danger-ous," he raised one brow at Margie to solicit her opinion, "but if you push him too far and he blows…"

Margie nodded slowly. "It has, unfortunately, been my experi-ence that everybody has a breaking point. You can drive anyone to violence if you push them hard enough. And Finkle was pretty distressed today. I thought at the time that it was just the discovery of a body in 'his' park and then seeing her picture. But it could also be due to a guilty conscience."

"We should dig a little deeper there. Maybe get him in for an interview. Check out his background, social media," Siever suggested. Margie had found his suggestions and careful documentation of their evidence to have been very helpful in the other cases she had worked on. He was a serious man, not as inclined as the others to joke and make sarcastic remarks. The kind of guy who tended to keep to himself most of the time, but was always watching and cataloging everything.

"Yeah. Definitely. Where are we on getting Patty's phone records? I'd like to start talking to some of her friends. And this should help us track down her family." She pushed the page of possible password details she'd had Warner write down into the middle of the table where others could see it. He might have denied knowing her friends' last names, but he had written down her parents' full names. No birth dates, but it was enough to get them started.

"We need to get a positive identification," Jones advised. "We're tracking down dental records. Without much help from Mr. Warner, I have to say. If we can get her electronics from him, she probably has her dentist in her contact list. He's probably right about her using one of the kids' names for her password. It's pretty common."

"Do you want to make arrangements to stop by the house and get them? I'm afraid if we wait for him, he's not going to move on it. Or he'll try to crack them at home and we'll lose important information."

"Sure," Jones agreed with a brisk nod. "No problem. I'll get over there right away."

"Okay, well…" Margie looked at the list of items to follow up on in her notepad. "We've got a lot to do, so we'll just keep moving things forward."

❦

It didn't feel like they had accomplished much at the end of the day, but Margie knew that she had been working hard on it ever since she'd received the call early that morning. It felt like she had been working for three days straight, so when MacDonald prompted her to go home and get some sleep so she'd be able to be productive on the case the next day, she admitted she was too exhausted to do anything else on it and packed things away.

Christina had beaten her home and had already eaten supper by the time Margie got there.

"I'm sorry," Margie apologized. "It's been a bear of a day."

Christina rolled her eyes but didn't complain about how that always seemed to happen and maybe it had something to do with Margie's choice to join the Calgary homicide department. Maybe things would have been quieter if she'd taken a different position, or moved to a small town instead of somewhere busier.

"I know. I'm saying that too often. Did you have something good for dinner? Was there enough in the fridge?" Margie opened the fridge and then the freezer, hoping to be inspired about what to make for her own dinner. The only thing that looked appetizing was the ice cream, and she had to be the adult and not be a bad example for her daughter. Eating ice cream for dinner was the wrong standard to set.

Christina grunted. "This and that. There was some leftover pizza."

Margie looked in the fridge. Christina had finished it off. Which was probably a good thing. Margie should eat something that was good for her. Lots of fruits and veggies. A salad, maybe. She shut the doors of the fridge again.

"There's pasta in the cupboard," Christina suggested. "Or, you could have a sandwich."

Probably the same things that Margie would have suggested to Christina. Kids were good at reflecting back what they heard from their parents at inopportune times. Margie opened the cupboards and eventually settled on a bowl of raisin bran. Christina watched as she poured a bowl and added milk.

"That's breakfast, not dinner."

"Today, it's dinner. Give me a break this one time."

Christina was silent, looking back down at her homework.

"How's it coming along?" Margie asked. "What are you working on?"

"Just… English… math…"

"You need any help?"

"No."

"Okay."

Christina didn't look up as she scratched out some math equations. "Are you going to tell me about the new case?"

"I can't really say much about it. A body was found at Ralph Klein Park."

"Is that near one of the other ones?"

"No. It's not far from here, actually. Driving, that is. Walking, it would be too far."

"Yeah? What's it like?"

"Wetlands. Lots of ponds and water catchments and canals or streams. There is a playground with a zip line and an education center to teach kids about the wetlands."

"Cool. We could take Stella there. She'd think it was great!"

Margie thought about Stella jumping into the big basin around the education center and shuddered. She wouldn't be able to jump in to pull Stella out if something happened to her.

"There were signs up that there aren't any dogs allowed in Ralph Klein Park. We'll take her to Glenbow one of these days. And go into Cochrane for ice cream." Margie glanced at the closed freezer door. She was definitely hung up on ice cream tonight.

"Yeah! I want to do that. I was talking to Stacey about Cochrane, and she says MacKay's is awesome. They have ice cream flavors like you never even thought of there, and it's always changing, so you can try new things."

"It sounds really cool. I want to see it too."

48

"*Cool*," Christina repeated with a grimace, picking up on the unintended pun.

Margie laughed. She continued to munch on her raisin bran.

"So, what else?" Christina asked.

"What else?"

"About your case. It was at Ralph Klein Park. Closer to us this time. But not anyone we know, right?" she asked lightly.

"No one we know involved in this case," Margie assured her quickly.

They didn't need more nightmares.

"Was it… like the others? Another stabbing?"

"No. I didn't see any marks on the body. The medical examiner will have to do the postmortem and report back, but it was probably a drowning."

Nothing that Christina wouldn't read in the news in the morning. If it hadn't already been reported.

"Do you know who did it?"

"No. We have some suspects. First, we need to conclusively identify the victim. We think we know who it is, but it takes some time to be absolutely sure. In the meantime, we're investigating all leads."

"You'll find him?"

"Calgary homicide has a very good solve rate. We'll find him."

"At least you didn't have to go in the water." Christina looked up from her notebook. "Right?"

"No. Not in the water." Margie couldn't suppress a shudder. "Just… close. And… over bridges." She didn't describe the walkways around the education center. She didn't want to picture them or remember them in any detail. She tried to block as much of that experience out as she could. Maybe, as Cruz said, the only way for her to get over her anxieties was through exposure to them, but that didn't mean she was going to dwell on them any more than she already had to.

"You went over a bridge?" Christina asked.

"Yes."

"In the car or on foot?"

"On foot. Actually, I had to go over one in the car too. But that was easier."

"Wow. Good for you." While Christina would laugh and tease Margie about her unreasonable fear of the water at other times, she always encouraged Margie to be brave and face her fears and try new things. Margie tried to do the same with Christina, encouraging her to do the things she was afraid of.

It was always easier to tell someone else to face their own fears than it was to face her own.

CHAPTER NINE

The next day Margie had a report from the medical examiner's office on her desk indicating that their victim had not had water in her lungs. She had not been drowned in the stream out at Ralph Klein Park.

Margie took a few deep breaths, her heart racing and stomach feeling queasy. Even though the medical examiner said that the woman had *not* died of drowning, she still couldn't help but imagine that cold, dark water flowing over her face, sealing off her mouth and nose, blinding her. She imagined sinking farther and farther down into the muck at the bottom of the stream, trying sluggishly to move, but being trapped like in a nightmare. Frozen, too afraid to even fight back against the water.

"Detective Pat...? Margie?"

Margie tried to break free of the vision. She wasn't drowning. The victim hadn't drowned. There wasn't any point to imagining it. She didn't want to see it, so why was she?

"Margie." There was a hand on her arm.

Margie opened her eyes and looked into Detective Jones's concerned blue eyes. She drew a deep breath. She could breathe just fine. She wasn't drowning. No one was drowning.

"It's okay. I'm okay."

"Are you sure? You were kind of… wheezing. Are you asthmatic? Do you need an inhaler?"

"No. I'm okay. I was just…" Margie trailed off, not wanting to have to explain it. "I'll tell you about it later. It's just… a distraction."

"You got the ME's report?" Jones nodded to it.

"Yes. Not drowning." Margie studied it for more details. "Several blows to the head. Subdural hematoma." She shook her head. "A fight… someone really got angry with her."

Jones sighed and shook her head, eyes closed. Margie thought about Finkle. Could he have snuck up on Patty? Approached her when she had been deep in thought or busy with something. Maybe not something quiet, like Margie had been picturing, but something noisy. The noise would distract her, cover up Finkle's footsteps. And then…

She couldn't see him sneaking up and bludgeoning her. That didn't make any sense. She tried again. An argument? A disagreement over something that had resulted in Patty throwing one of her insults in Finkle's face? Not behind his back, this time, but face-to-face, so that he couldn't deny it. Couldn't pretend that his staff respected him.

A slur or insult that had pricked him to act. It was too much, and he had just picked up the nearest possible weapon and slugged her with it. Repeatedly. Or he had knocked her down and continued to beat her.

In those scenarios, Patty would have to have been the last one there with him at the end of the day. So that no one else had seen or heard what had happened, or observed him disposing of the body.

Would Finkle have disposed of the body in the waterways of his beloved park? Would he have thought it fitting to return her to nature and to bury her in the water that she too had been so passionate about? Or would he think that was polluting the waters that they were trying to purify by running through the natural filters of the wetlands?

"They were both passionate about nature," Margie mused aloud. "What could they have fought about?"

"Who?"

"Patty and Finkle." Margie closed her eyes, thinking about it for a minute. It wouldn't have been because Finkle had propositioned Patty, something that happened in many workplaces. If she and the others thought that he was in the closet, then he clearly wasn't sexually harassing the women who worked under him. Unless it was to overcompensate. To make them think that he was just as big a pig as any other man who had ever abused them.

"Did we get the ID?"

"Dental clinic near her house. They're sending over x-rays. ME should have a positive ID by the end of the day."

"Good." Margie was relieved about that. She didn't want Patty's family and friends to be wondering any longer than necessary about what had happened to her. They deserved to have a little peace, knowing that she was not suffering. Knowing was better.

"Multiple blows," Jones mused, skimming the ME's report over Margie's shoulder. "Torn nails and defensive bruises on her hands. Broken finger. It was a fight. She didn't just go down with one blow."

"No." Margie pictured Finkle. Had he had any scratches or bruises on his hands? He'd been constantly wringing them. Margie had spent a lot of time looking at them, winding and squeezing each other. She was pretty sure she would have noticed if he'd had any bruising on his hands.

But then, if he'd used some kind of an object as a bludgeon, he wouldn't have bruised his hands.

There could have been someone else at work, someone who had propositioned her, or someone she had been having an affair with. Someone bigger and more explosive than Finkle.

"We need to talk to her family and friends. See if she and Warner had marital issues. See if they knew about the situation at work. Or if she'd been under more stress lately. Finkle said that she had been moody. Why?"

She remembered what else Finkle had said. He'd thought that maybe she was hormonal. Maybe pregnant. She flipped through the pages of the ME's report, scanning the rest of the information. She shook her head. No pregnancy. That was something, at least. It would have been worse—or at least, felt worse—if Patty had been pregnant when she was killed.

"I'm going to make some calls," she told Jones. "I know we don't have a confirmed ID yet, but I want to start talking to others before they know too much. People start to make things up. They start to imagine the reasons things happened the way they did. I don't want confabulation. I want the facts."

"Sure. Do you want me to make some calls?"

"We'll start with Mom and Dad. They can let us know who else we should be talking to."

"All right. The contact details we were able to pull are in the workspace. Interview room is yours as long as you want it."

Margie appreciated Detective Jones taking care of these little details and smoothing the way for Margie's investigation.

"You want to sit in with me?"

"Sure, if you want. That won't be too many people?"

"No, I don't think so. I think they'll feel better if they feel like more people are involved in seeing that justice is served."

CHAPTER TEN

*B*ecause Patty was estranged from her parents, they hadn't known she was missing before Margie's call. Margie invited them to talk to her, telling them as little as possible. Certainly not that she was with the homicide department. Let them think, at least for a little while, that Patty had just not gone home for one night. There could be a perfectly reasonable explanation for that.

Their eyes were wide and frightened when Margie met them in the reception area. She took them to the interview room. Nothing between the lobby and the interview room indicated to the couple that they were dealing with homicide rather than with missing persons. They were both housed in the same building and on the same floor. Only the room numbers gave it away to those who knew those little details.

"Mr. and Mrs. Roscoe, thank you for coming in. I'm sorry to have to involve you in this."

Mrs. Roscoe was wiping her nose with a well-used tissue. Face masks were not an option when people were crying. Margie gave them a box of tissues and a garbage can and sat at the other side of the table, her own mask firmly in place.

"Is she really missing?" Mrs. Roscoe asked. "My baby!"

"I know it must be a shock to you. This is something that no parent ever wants to hear."

"No," she agreed. Mr. Roscoe shook his head, blinking his eyes rapidly.

"When was the last time you saw or talked to your daughter?"

"Well... it's been a long time, actually. I don't know if anyone told you..." Mrs. Roscoe looked down at the table, her face pink with shame. "We were not talking with each other. Things were not good between us." Tears escaped her eyes and flooded down her cheeks. "Why couldn't we have made up before now? I don't even know when the last time we talked to each other was."

"Did you have any communication at all? Texts or emails?"

"No. I still saw her social media posts sometimes. But... well, I didn't respond to them."

"I understand. What was it the two of you fell out over?"

"Her husband. That Scott. Scott Warner. I suppose he told you all about it."

"No, he didn't have much to say about it. I think he would have preferred not to have talked about it at all. But I told him I would be talking with you, so he might as well fill me in because I was going to hear it from you anyway."

She nodded. "What did he tell you? About how unreasonable and judging we are, I suppose. That we never gave him a chance."

"Why don't you tell me in your own words?"

The couple exchanged glances. Mrs. Roscoe was the one who was more comfortable talking, but maybe she felt that her husband would sound more reasonable. Logical rather than emotional like she was.

"Just take your time," Margie urged. "I'm listening."

Mrs. Roscoe turned back to her and began reluctantly. "He just wasn't any good. I knew from the start that he wasn't going to amount to anything. I can't for the life of me imagine what she saw in the man. It wasn't even like he was good looking, so she couldn't say that it was his looks or love at first sight."

But she wasn't judging Warner.

"What made you think that he wasn't good for your daughter? They didn't have shared interests?"

"He's a bum. Patty is the one who has had to support that family from the start."

"He has a job, from what I understood."

"Yes. A job. But no education. Patty is the one who has always made the lion's share of the family's income. He should have just stayed home with the kids; then they wouldn't have had to pour money into daycare. But no, he couldn't do that either. He had to have a career. He had to show everyone that he could amount to something."

Margie made a couple of notes. "So, your concerns were mostly financial?"

"No, not just that. He wasn't a nice person. Isn't. I'm sure that hasn't changed. I didn't want him anywhere near Patty. Or my grandchildren."

"In what way wasn't he nice?" Margie didn't want to suggest that they had argued or that there had been any violence in the family. She didn't want to feed them anything. Let them offer it on their own.

"He was always talking down to her. Like he was the one who had the university education rather than her. He acted like she was... inferior. He was more intelligent, understood politics and the world economy better than she did. He thought he was naturally smart; he didn't need book learning. In fact, he was better without it. Less tainted."

"Really. A know-it-all. They can be very annoying."

"Yes. No one else ever knows anything. If you do, then you're wrong. He has to correct everything you say, and make sure everyone knows that he is the one who gets it all, that he's some-how... an advanced species over everyone else around him."

Margie nodded.

"That might be an exaggeration," Mr. Roscoe temporized. His wife gave him a withering glare. "I don't think it was that bad," Mr. Roscoe said. "At least... not that obvious. The two of them usually seemed to get along pretty well. She allowed him to express his opinions and didn't try to correct him and make him feel bad about the stuff he got wrong. She was very patient with him."

"A wife shouldn't have to be patient with her husband. Not like that. She shouldn't always have to tiptoe around his ego and make him think he's better than she is. That's just wrong."

"It seemed to work okay for them. They didn't fight a lot. Not around us."

"They were never around us," Mrs. Roscoe said. "I saw him for what he was in the beginning, and I said I wouldn't be around them."

Mr. Roscoe gave a nod and shrug. He clearly didn't find Warner quite as objectionable as his wife did. Maybe because he was a man and felt a certain kinship to him in his situation that his wife couldn't feel. Perhaps he could see how Warner might feel in a marriage with a stronger, more outspoken woman. Or maybe his wife was just better at picking up on the subtleties of Patty's and Warner's relationship.

"You must have seen her sometimes. Did you go to her wedding? See the children when they were born or at other times?"

"They had a civil ceremony and didn't see fit to invite us to that," Mrs. Roscoe said stiffly. Another problem that she had with Warner. "When the children were born... Yes, I did go by the hospital to see them when that man was not there. But the rest of the time..." She closed her eyes and shook her head slowly. "I didn't see them. Didn't babysit for them or have family dinners together." She swallowed and dabbed at tears. "I should have made up with her when I had the chance. Now... it's too late. She's gone. Thinking I didn't care."

"She knew you cared," Mr. Roscoe told her, putting his hand over hers. "She knew that the reason you didn't want her with Scott was that you did love her and wanted her to be happy."

But it had probably not made her happy to have to choose between the two of them. Or not to have her mother in her life.

"So if you haven't seen them lately, and didn't have anything to do with them regularly, then I don't suppose there is anything you can tell me about their relationship. Or whether she was under any new stresses the last little while."

"No… we just weren't a part of her life anymore," Mrs. Roscoe said. "I was… waiting for her to see the light and to leave him."

Margie sincerely hoped that wasn't what had resulted in Patty's death.

"How long had she worked at the park?" she tried. "Do you know anything about how she enjoyed that? Whether she got along with everybody she worked with?"

"She's been working there since she got out of school. She liked it. At least, she did back then. I don't know if she's had any problems since then. I guess if she's still there, she must like it. Otherwise, she would have left by now."

"Do you remember anything about her coworkers? I know it has been a few years since you would have heard anything about them, but is there anything you remember?"

"No… not really. There were always other students or recent graduates working there. Lots of young people her age. So it was comfortable for her, lots of people she could relate to."

"And her bosses or supervisors? They must have been older than her."

"She talked about them sometimes… everybody has frustrations with supervisors at work. Policies and procedures. Getting to work late. Trying to get a raise after a positive performance review. You know how it is."

"Of course," Margie agreed. "Was she not advancing as fast as she had hoped?"

"I think all kids think they're going to change the world. She thought she could walk in there and make a difference. Teach them all of the things she had learned in school. But you can't just walk into a place as the newest employee and update all of their procedures, implement all of the latest science. It takes time and experience."

Margie nodded. "After five years, or however long she has worked there, hopefully she was able to put some of her ideas into action. I guess you wouldn't know…"

The two of them shook their heads. There was a lot of sadness in Mrs. Roscoe's face. Not just grief over whatever had happened to her daughter, but the realization that she had missed out on her daughter's life the last few years when she didn't have to. If it had been Margie, she would also be wondering what would happen to the children and whether she would ever see them again. If something had happened to Patty—as they had to guess it had—then what were the chances that Warner would allow them to be a part of the grandchildren's lives?

§

Mrs. Roscoe had been able to provide some of the names of Patty's friends, at least the ones she had spent time with before getting married. And she had Patty's email address, even though they didn't still correspond with each other. Assuming Patty was still using the same email address, it gave them not only a chance to get into her email, but also her cloud storage and syncing. If they couldn't guess her password on the first few tries, they could get a subpoena for the service provider once the identification was verified.

"Do we have confirmation on the dental records yet?" she asked the team in general as she returned to the duty room after finishing with the Roscoes.

"Dr. Galt says it is a match," Siever confirmed. "He'll get us his official report later today."

"Yes!" Margie had harbored the secret worry that they were going in completely the wrong direction and they would find, on comparing the dental records, that it wasn't Patty Roscoe at all. "I mean, that's terrible, but at least we have a name now. Did we get the devices?" She looked over at Jones.

"We did." Jones pulled down her face mask for a moment and grimaced. "Hubby claimed not to know the unlock password on the tablet, but it looks to me like it's been sanitized. I'll send it over to the lab to have them see if they can recover anything. It's possible that she was just using it as an e-reader, but most people will at least put their email on the thing."

"She might have just used it as an entertainment device for the kids too," Cruz offered. "That's mostly what my wife's gets used for. Electronic babysitter when she has to stand in line for something. If the kids are going to be playing on it, you don't want them to have access to your email or schedule or anything else that they could end up messing around with."

"That's a possibility," Jones admitted. "It does have Netflix Kids and Disney+ on it."

Cruz nodded. Jones swore under her breath, not happy about this. "I've got her laptop as well. Hopefully, it has better security and he didn't guess her password before I got it from him. I don't trust the guy."

"I have a few friends to run down," Margie said, looking down at her notepad. "I'm hoping some of them were still in close touch with Patty. And then I might have another talk with Finkle. I have a feeling he wasn't totally honest with us."

CHAPTER ELEVEN

*T*he calls with Patty's friends did not go as well as she had hoped. They were old friends, but had not had a lot to do with Patty during the last few years. They had gone different directions, had different friends, and most were still single or childless. One woman who did have a child only had a baby, none close to Patty's children's ages. So they hadn't spent much time together recently.

They expressed the appropriate shock that Patty was missing and something might have happened to her. Margie tried to gently broach the possibility that her husband might have had something to do with it with each of them, but didn't have much success.

"Do you know her husband, Scott Warner?" she asked Mindy, the one with a baby.

"Oh, we've met. I don't know him well, but he seems like a nice guy."

"You didn't ever think that he and Patty might be having problems?"

"We didn't see much of each other," Mindy reminded her. "I didn't see them together a lot. But she didn't complain about him that I heard. And when they were together, or I could hear him in the background, I never thought he was being an—well, I thought he seemed like a nice enough guy. They didn't fight or snipe at each other in front of me. He didn't tell her she was stupid or push her around."

"You didn't find him critical or argumentative?" Margie asked, thinking of what Mrs. Roscoe had said.

"Well, he was a man. Of course he was argumentative. Wanted to make sure you heard his side of the story and knew that he was the expert on everything. But that's kind of par for the course with guys like him."

"Like him?"

"Well…" Mindy looked for a word. "Kind of… guys who think they're smart? Have all of the answers, even if they change from one day to the next."

"A know-it-all?"

"Yeah. Like that. But not… I wasn't scared of him. He wasn't threatening or the kind that would get all hot and bang the table if you disagreed with him. Just… he wanted you to know how smart he was."

Margie thought about Oscar. He had wanted her to know how smart he was, too. Couldn't stand the thought that a woman might be more intelligent than he was.

§

MARGIE LOOKED DOWN at her phone. She wanted to get some more work done, but she'd been on the phone for hours. Her ear was hot and sore. Christina would soon be arriving home from school, and Margie didn't want her to be on her own for too long. She could continue her investigation from home. There were other people she could call or email, some research and background she needed to do. She still hadn't talked to Finkle again, but she suspected that he would be leaving the park soon if he hadn't gone home already, and she hadn't asked him for his personal number. With a sigh, she started to put her things away.

"Heading out?" MacDonald asked, startling Margie as he came up from behind her somewhere.

Margie caught her breath and pressed her hand over her racing heart. "Yes. I'll do some more from home, but I want to see my daughter—"

"Don't take your work home with you. Go home and relax and spend time with your family. Come fresh in the morning. You'll be more productive if you balance it out and take breaks than if you try to push through. You can't keep up that pace every day. We'll run this guy down, but it's going to be slow and steady, not a race. We'll eliminate suspects, process evidence, dig into the history. It's not all going to happen in a day."

Margie paused and considered his words. "I *have* been putting in a lot of hours on this."

"And you need to take care of yourself. You've had three back-to-back leads since you arrived here. You're going to burn out if you don't give yourself recovery time."

"Okay." Margie nodded. "All right. I'll take tonight off. I won't do anything. Just take some time with my family."

Mac nodded. "Good. We'll see you tomorrow morning, bright-eyed and ready to get back to it."

It was like physically training for a race or building muscle. Margie needed the rest days and breaks in between to be alert enough to see what was in front of her.

❧

CHRISTINA WAS LYING on her bed, chatting on her phone when Margie got home. She rolled over and looked at her mother, eyebrows raised.

"Just a minute," she said to her friend, and covered the phone. "What are you doing home?"

"I wanted to spend some time with you. I know I've been working too late the last couple of nights."

"Nice."

"I didn't even bring anything home with me. I have a free night. I can cook while you're doing your homework, and then we can do what we want. Take Stella out for a long walk. Run some errands—"

"Go visit Moushoom?"

"Sure, of course. I'm sure he'd be happy to see us again."

Christina nodded. She returned to her phone call. "My mom is home," she said in an exasperated voice. "I have to do homework."

Margie was taken aback for a moment at this change in attitude. Then she laughed to herself. Christina just didn't want whoever she was talking with to think that she was uncool, wanting to spend time with her mother and Moushoom. Teenagers weren't supposed to care about that. They were supposed to be all about gaming and streaming video and social media. Margie went into the kitchen and looked through the fridge, this time with an eye to actually cooking something rather than just feeding a craving for sugar at the end of a stressful day. Salad, maybe a stir fry and rice. Maybe Christina would want some tofu or one of the various vegetarian meats they had purchased to try out.

If she had enough vegetables for dinner, maybe she wouldn't feel like dessert afterward. Her belt was starting to feel just a touch tight, and she didn't want to let her weight get away from her. She might not be a beat cop anymore, but that didn't mean she didn't have to keep up her fitness level. She never knew when she might have to run or get a combative suspect under control.

Christina came into the kitchen. She gave Margie a sideways hug, also gazing into the fridge. "Some noodles too?" she suggested. "We can make lo mein?"

"Okay, sure."

They busied themselves getting the ingredients out and fell into a rhythm chopping vegetables.

"How was school?"

"Oh, you know. It sucked. And then it was over."

Margie chuckled. "Who was on the phone? I don't know about any of your new friends."

"Tracy."

"Tracy. Is she the one who was telling you about MacKay's?"

"No, that was Stacey."

"Oh. Who is Tracy? What is she like?"

"He."

"What?" Margie looked up at her. "He? Tracy?"

"Yes."

"The poor guy. Who names their son Tracy in this day and age?"

"I guess there used to be a lot of guys named Tracy. Before it became a girl name. Seems like people are always giving their girls boy names, but then all of the guys with that name end up being judged as being feminine."

"Yes, it was used more a couple of generations ago. But now... I didn't think anyone would pick it for a boy name."

"Well..." Christina popped the end of a carrot in her mouth. "He's Chinese, actually, and his family adopted English names to make them fit in better. So they let the kids pick their own names. And he didn't know then that it was kind of a girly name now. He just picked it out of a book or off of a website of boy names."

"Well... it's nice he was allowed to pick his own name, but maybe they could let him pick a new one now. He doesn't have to make it his legal name if he doesn't want to, just something else for people to call him."

"I think he'll probably just go back to his Chinese name. Plenty of the Chinese kids around here go by their Chinese names and never adopted an English name."

Margie held her cutting board over the wok and slid the chopped vegetables into it. They immediately started to sizzle. "That's good. I don't think people should have to pick another name because they're from another culture. Canada isn't supposed to be a melting pot like the States. It's supposed to be a cultural mosaic. So why not keep your cultural name?"

Christina nodded her agreement. "Is that why you never changed Marguerite to Margaret?"

"It's a very common Métis name. It's not hard to remember or pronounce, so I don't see any reason to change it."

"Do people give you a lot of hassle about Patenaude?"

"I get a lot of 'Detective Pat.' It's easier for people, and I don't mind. They don't make fun of it." Margie stopped to read the instructions on the faux meat package that Christina had taken out of the fridge. "Do you get hassled for it at school?"

"No. People ask how to pronounce it or spell it, but a lot of the names are weirder than Patenaude. The Asian ones with too many consonants that we would put vowels between. It isn't like I have a name that's ten syllables long."

Margie was relieved that Christina wasn't being bullied over her name. She had been worried, going from Winnipeg to Calgary, with such different demographics, that their Métis culture would cause friction. And there would still be a few people who were jerks about it. That went without saying. But it wasn't like Christina was the only dark-skinned girl in a sea of white. The school was full of kids with all different shades of skin, from redheads with starkly white skin or freckles to ebony black with a blue sheen that she had rarely ever seen in Manitoba. Margie had been pleased with the diversity.

CHAPTER TWELVE

It was still light enough when they got to Moushoom's apartment to ask him if he wanted to go out for a walk with them. He loved to get out into the fresh air and nature whenever they could take him. The old Métis man always looked like a painting to Margie. He dressed in a mix of traditional clothes, including buckskins and a sash, and store-bought clothing like the long-sleeved boldly-colored dress shirts and dark sunglasses that he loved. Despite a long life full of tragedies and sorrow, his deep wrinkles seemed to always point up in a smile. She could have stared at him for hours and wished she had the skill to draw or paint him how he appeared to her.

"I want kisses from my two favorite girls," Moushoom declared, making them lean down to embrace him and kissing them on both cheeks, despite the pandemic. "I'm so glad that you came to live in Calgary."

"Me too," Margie told him. "It's wonderful to be so close to you."

"Do you want to go out?" Christina asked, looking through the clothes in Moushoom's closet. "You will need a jacket."

"Yes, let's go out," he agreed. He patted Margie's arm. "She is getting so big."

"Isn't she? I can't believe it sometimes. It seems like she was a little baby just yesterday."

"She is a woman now."

Christina found a jacket that she deemed suitable for their outing. It was blue with contrasting white stitching and beadwork. "This is beautiful." She helped Moushoom to get it on, then took charge of the wheelchair, releasing his brakes and pointing the chair toward the door. Moushoom folded his hands in his lap and smiled.

A few years ago, he would have insisted on getting around under his own power. He would have walked, no matter how much it cost him later. It gave Margie a little pang of pain to realize how he'd had to accept his physical limitations. He had been such a strong and active person for so many years. Now he was shrinking and becoming more dependent. That was the way of life, but she didn't like seeing him getting weaker.

She pasted a smile on her face and didn't show what she was thinking. There was nothing to be done about advancing age. All they could do was enjoy the time that they had together the best they could.

Moushoom took a deep breath when they got outside. "It was warm today," he observed. "You never know at this time of year whether it will be warm or cold."

"We had frost last week," Margie said. "And it was rainy and smoky the beginning of the week, but today was warm."

"And sometimes we have a foot of snow mid-September." Moushoom shrugged. "It has been nice so far this year."

"It has," Margie agreed.

"Where did you go this week?" Moushoom asked.

"Where did I go?" Margie wasn't sure what he meant. "Umm… I've just been here in Calgary. I went to work."

"No park this week? You were telling me all about that big park last time."

"Oh. No, I haven't been out to Glenbow Park again yet. I want to take you and Christina and Stella out there soon. When it's a nice day. We can take a tour. They have golf cart tours, so you don't have to walk and we don't have to push your wheelchair up the hill."

"I'm light."

"It's a big hill!"

"Who is Stella?" Moushoom studied her. "You only have one daughter."

"Stella is our dog."

"Oh, yes," Moushoom nodded and chuckled. "She is the dog. You didn't bring her?"

"Not today. I wasn't sure if we were allowed to bring her into the building or if you would want to go out today."

"You can bring her into the building. Some of the people there have dogs of their own."

"Great! We'll bring her next time, then."

They walked for a few minutes in silence.

"I did go to a different park this week," Margie offered. "Have you ever heard of Ralph Klein Park?"

He shook his head. "Another new one? I remember Ralph Klein. He's dead, isn't he?"

"Yes. That's probably why they named a park after him. They don't usually do it while the person is still alive."

"Is it a good park?"

"Umm… I didn't get to explore it much. It's not big, like Glenbow or Fish Creek."

"It has water," Christina offered. "Mom was saying that it is a wetlands park, so it has a bunch of ponds and streams."

"Wetlands are good," Moushoom said, licking his lips. "The white man destroyed too many of them. Why they think it's a good idea to wipe out the natural habitat and replace it with concrete, I'll never understand." He motioned to the development around them. In a minute, they would be onto the pathway beside the irrigation canal, and he would be much happier. Even though it was only a narrow strip of land, it was better than being surrounded by concrete and buildings. And on a good day, they could look out past the city to the mountains. There was too much smoke in the air for them to see anything today. But hopefully, it would dissipate in the next few days.

"One of the girls is afraid of water," Moushoom said. "Which girl is that?" He turned his head to look at Christina, pushing his chair. "Is it you?"

"No." Christina smiled at him. "It's Mom."

"You?" Moushoom looked at Margie. "Is it you? I couldn't remember."

"Yes," Margie admitted. Her face got warm, but between her complexion and the dimming light, she didn't think he would be able to tell she was embarrassed. "It's me. I know it's silly, but it's not by choice."

"We don't get to choose what we fear," Moushoom agreed. "We can choose how to behave in the face of our fears, but we do not get to pick our fears."

Margie nodded.

"You are not limited by your fears," Moushoom went on. "You live a full life."

Was it an observation or a command? Was he pleased that she didn't let her fear limit her, or was he telling her not to?

"I try to," she told him.

"Good." He reached out to pat her hand, then looked on ahead toward the green space, his expression softening, mouth going slightly slack. She didn't try to draw him into conversation, letting him think about whatever it was he was remembering or imagining.

CHAPTER THIRTEEN

*M*argie felt relaxed and clearheaded the next morning as she drove in to work. She was glad she had listened to Mac and put her work aside for the night. The time with Christina and Moushoom, and later on her own without any agenda, had helped. She had slept well and woke up feeling like a new person.

She listened to a classic rock station on the way downtown, enjoying the music and ignoring the DJs' chatter. Other days, when she was stressed, she couldn't stand to hear their drivel.

Margie was energized by her morning coffee and dove into her work, quickly reviewing her notes from the day before and any new information that had been uploaded into the workspace for the case. Not a lot had been done since the time she had left, which was probably good because overworking the lab or medical examiner's office was not a good idea either. Everybody deserved to get their rest.

Her eyes were on her computer screen and she didn't look to see who was calling before answering the ringing phone.

"Detective Patenaude."

"Detective! This is Carol Roscoe." Patty's mother's voice was high-pitched. She sounded panicked.

Margie winced. If Dr. Galt had issued his official identification of Patty Roscoe, as Margie assumed that he had, then she was going to have to inform Mr. and Mrs. Roscoe that their daughter was dead, as they had feared. Or maybe Mrs. Roscoe already knew. Had someone else informed her? Or had the news been leaked, and she had found out on social media or the morning news? She was definitely not in the same place emotionally as she had been the day before.

"Mrs. Roscoe. I'm glad you called," she said, in a voice intended to soothe Mrs. Roscoe. Half of the battle was making a caller feel heard. She would find out the reason Mrs. Roscoe had called and, hopefully, leave her in a better place than she had found her.

"I got an email," Mrs. Roscoe said, her voice wild, cracking up and down like an adolescent's. "An email from Patty!"

Margie blinked, staring at the screen in front of her and trying to figure out if she had heard correctly. "I'm sorry. You got an email about Patty?"

"No, from Patty. I got an email from Patty."

"I don't think that's possible, Mrs. Roscoe."

"I did!"

"What does it say?"

"There is a video recording attached. A video of Arabella."

Arabella. It took a couple of seconds for Margie to remember that was one of Patty's daughters. The older one, if she remembered correctly.

"So did this email come from Arabella?" Margie queried. "Have you ever gotten anything from the girls before?"

"You need to listen to it. Something has happened to Patty. Something... I knew that Scott was no good. I told you. I told Patty. She always said that I was wrong and he was perfectly good to her, but I knew she wasn't telling me the truth. He was mean and manipulative. He kept her from me."

Mrs. Roscoe seemed to be forgetting the fact that she was the one who had cut off communications from Patty.

"I would be happy to listen to it. Do you want to forward it to me? I'll give you my email address."

Mrs. Roscoe covered up the phone to talk to someone else, her voice going muffled. Margie could still just make her words out. "Do you know how to forward this?"

"What's the address?" Mr. Roscoe answered.

"She's going to give it to me."

The phone was taken from her. "Detective?" Mr. Roscoe asked.

"Yes, I'm here."

"What's your email address? Am I supposed to send this to you?"

"Yes, if you could." Margie gave him her email address as slowly and clearly as she could.

"Okay, I'm sending it to you now." There was a click, and Mr. Roscoe was gone.

Margie shook her head. She pressed the Send/Receive button on her email client and waited to see if it would appear. He might have taken her address down wrong. Or pushed the wrong button and it was still sitting in his drafts folder. Or it might just be taking time to process, if it had a video attached. As much as she expected email to be instantaneous, she knew that it still took time to get from one place to another.

She clicked Send/Receive again and waited.

The third time she refreshed, a bolded message appeared in her inbox. Margie double-clicked it, and then clicked on the video attachment.

The picture was fuzzy, the little girl too close to the device and not pointing it directly at herself. She was talking to herself in a whisper. Margie turned it up, plugged in earphones, and rewound to start it over again. She leaned toward the computer as if that might make the picture and words clearer.

"Mommy said do Gramma's picture," Arabella whispered. "The red button then the Gramma button. Send a message."

Margie blinked, watching it. Did Arabella have Patty's phone?

An iPod of her own? A burner phone for emergency calls? Arabella was clearly talking herself through whatever instructions her mother had given her previously.

Arabella looked up, away from the phone, listening or watching something else. Her face came into focus for a few seconds. There were tears on her face. Red blotches. Her pudgy fist wiped away some of the tear tracks. Her nose blew a snot bubble. There was background noise. Margie turned the system volume up as far as it would go. She could hear voices in the background. Two voices, a man and a woman. The TV? Scott Warner and a visitor in another room? Margie tried to make out the words, but could only catch a phrase here and there. There was a crashing noise that drowned everything else out, screaming that made the hair on the back of Margie's neck stand on end, and Arabella's hands both flew up to her face, the camera getting buried in the blankets of her bed. There was a male voice shouting, Arabella crying softly to herself, and then the video ended.

Margie stared at the end frame in confusion.

"Detective Siever?" She called across the duty room to him. He looked up from his screen.

"Uh-huh?"

"I... I..." Margie stared at her screen, trying to form the question in her mind. She shook her head. "Can you help me with something?"

He got up from his desk, exhaling noisily. His chair creaked as he pushed himself to his feet. "Yeah? What is it?" he asked as he approached her desk.

"This video... it doesn't make any sense. Is it possible that... could that be Patty Roscoe in the background?"

"I thought the ME had a positive identification on her."

"Me too. That's why... I'm not sure I understand what's going on here."

He bent over and pressed play on the video. Margie switched it from her headphones to the external speaker. The bullpen quieted around them as everybody listened. Margie was even more sure the second time. It had to be Patty and her husband in the background. Arguing, and then… was it possible they had a recording of the murder?

"Where did this come from?" Siever asked.

"It came from Patty's mother. She said she got it in an email from Patty. The little girl recorded it."

"And then she didn't send it until today," Siever said. "Or else the device didn't have a connection until today, so it was sitting in the queue waiting."

"Is there any way to tell when the video was recorded?"

Using her mouse and leaning over Margie's shoulder, the other detective clicked around, examining the email and the attached file.

"I'm going to send it to forensics and get them to look at it," he said. "But it looks like it was recorded a few days ago."

"The day of the murder?"

His eyes went to the stand-up calendar on Margie's desk, counting through the days. He nodded. "Yes."

Margie swore under her breath. "That poor girl. No wonder Warner didn't want us talking to them. Did he know that Arabella overheard them?"

"Even if he didn't, they would have known their mother had been home the night before. That his story of her never coming home was a lie. Now, a few days later, he's covered. A little girl that young isn't going to be able to tell us which day she saw her mother last. And even if she could, he could just say she was confused."

"This is enough to arrest him. I'll let MacDonald know." She looked at her watch. "Warner will be at his workplace. That's good. We can arrest him while he is away from the girls, no chance of him taking them hostage."

"Have them picked up from the daycare."

"Yes," Margie agreed. "They can go to the grandparents, at least initially. Oh, I'd better call them back. Poor Mrs. Roscoe is in a state."

"I would be too," Jones contributed from where she was sitting at her desk.

"Yeah." Margie tried not to think about the sound of Patty's scream. The more she reviewed it, the stronger it would be in her memory. She needed to stay focused on her next actions rather than what she had heard and the emotional impact. Compartmentalize and not think about how this was going to affect the Roscoe family and the little girls. "Me too."

She got up and walked over to MacDonald's office in the corner. His door was closed, and she hadn't noticed whether he was in or not. She pulled out her phone and called Mrs. Roscoe back while she tried to peer through MacDonald's blinds to see whether he was in.

"Mrs. Roscoe?"

The woman cried on the other end, not managing to get out anything coherent.

"You don't have to talk right now," Margie told her. "I'm just letting you know that I got the email and have watched the video. We're going to take action on it right away. We'll arrest Scott Warner. We're going to pick the girls up from their daycare. Are you home, and are you prepared to take them for a few days?"

Mrs. Roscoe sobbed and managed a shaky "Yes."

"Okay. We'll talk later."

CHAPTER FOURTEEN

*M*argie hung up and slid the phone back into her pocket. She knocked on MacDonald's door, looking into the bullpen at the other detectives. "Is he in? I wasn't paying attention earlier."

She was answered by MacDonald's voice from within. "Come in."

Margie opened the door and stuck her head in. Mac was sitting at his desk, phone in hand, muffling the receiver against his shoulder.

"Detective Patenaude. A break in the case?"

"Yes. It was the husband. We have enough for an arrest."

His eyebrows went way up. "What did you find?" They certainly hadn't been expecting to come across any evidence that would be that decisive.

"One of the little girls recorded a video the night of the murder. You can hear the parents arguing in the background. Hear a physical altercation and Patty screaming."

"That doesn't necessarily establish murder. There might have been any number of fights."

"I think… when you hear the video, you will agree. Detective Siever is forwarding it to forensics, and they'll verify the data on when it was recorded to make sure it lines up with the time of death. But even before they do that, we have enough to bring him in. It proves that, at the very least, he was physically abusive."

"If you can establish that it's him on the video. Does his face appear?"

"No. But you can hear them in the background. I recognize his voice."

MacDonald nodded. "Okay. Bring him in for questioning. We'll get the details on the video verified as soon as possible."

"Great. Will do. And we're going to have the girls picked up from the daycare; they can stay with their grandma for the time being."

But when she returned to the duty room, Jones shook her head grimly.

"They're not at the daycare. Warner didn't bring them in today."

Margie looked at her phone to verify that it wasn't the weekend. "Why didn't he take them to daycare today? That means… they're with him. He must not have work today."

The other detectives on the team gathered closer to work it through.

"He's not making funeral arrangements," Margie said, thinking aloud, "because we haven't informed him that we have an ID yet. He has to pretend he doesn't know she's dead."

"So he's taking a personal day," Cruz said. "What husband wouldn't take a day or two off when his wife goes missing? It would look suspicious if he didn't."

Margie nodded. "Then he's at home. Do you think?" She was worried about the video. What if he found out about it from Arabella? What if Mr. Roscoe decided to go over there to confront him? Now that they knew without a doubt that Warner was the killer, Margie was afraid something was going to go wrong before they could take him into custody. "Do you think he's just at home? Having a lazy day with the kids?"

The detectives looked at each other. Margie was sure they were going through scenarios in their heads, just as she was.

"Cleaning up, maybe," Siever suggested. "Going over the floor with bleach another time. Making sure that anything that got broken during the fight has been disposed of. And whatever he used as a bludgeon. He's got to know that we'll want to search the house once we have identified her."

"I'll call him," Margie decided. "I'll let him know that we've identified the body of his wife. We should be able to tell by the background noise whether he's at home or somewhere else."

No one disagreed with her suggestion. He had to be notified anyway. It wasn't going to come as a surprise, though they'd see how good an actor he was when he heard about it and faked a breakdown.

Margie sat back down at her desk and picked up her phone. She breathed a few times, slowing her respiration and distancing herself from the situation. It was just a notification. She'd done dozens of them before. She was able to separate herself from it emotionally. It was her job to figure out where he was. She needed to be able to make a snap judgment.

She hit the speakerphone button before placing the call so that the others would be able to hear too. More ears were better. Warner might be able to tell that she had him on speaker, but he was going to have to deal with that. She tapped in his number and waited for him to pick up.

All she got was a long period of ringing, followed by his voicemail.

"We'd better get over there," Margie said, hanging up. She didn't want to rush into anything, but the thought of the murderer with two young children in the house set her heart thumping at a much faster speed than usual. "Maybe he's just ignoring my call, or washing the floor like Siever says, but those children are defenseless. I have to make sure they're okay."

"You want me to go with you?" Jones offered.

"Uh, yes. But separate vehicles. If he bolts, I want to be able to stay on him. One of us."

Jones nodded. They both removed their sidearms from their lockboxes without comment and vested up. Who knew if he had an illegal weapon and would decide to do something stupid like holing up in his house and trying to shoot anyone who got too close?

"You two be careful," Cruz advised, even though it was obvious that they were taking the proper precautions.

"We will," Margie confirmed.

"At the first sign of trouble, you call for help and fall back. Don't push a confrontation."

She and Jones both nodded. Margie expected him to try to trade places with Jones to go along, but he didn't.

"Cover all exits. If it is an apartment building, call for backup."

"Yes."

Margie finished getting ready. She looked at him for any further advice. He just nodded. "Okay. You got this."

CHAPTER FIFTEEN

*M*argie's heart was beating so fast as she drove to Warner's address that it felt like it would burst right out of her chest. She didn't feel like she had it covered by any stretch of the imagination. So many things could go wrong.

But it could all go fine too. She might just be overreacting. Warner hadn't uttered any threats when she had interviewed him previously. He hadn't said or done anything that showed a propensity for violence. He hadn't argued, called her names, insisted that they needed to drop everything else and get on top of his wife's case. While there was an estrangement from Patty's parents that he acknowledged was due to their not liking him, Mr. and Mrs. Roscoe had not suggested that they thought him capable of violence toward her or the children. She'd left the conversation wide open for them to make whatever claims they chose to. Warner had no domestic violence charges, no previous calls to the house over noise complaints or neighbor concerns. She hadn't checked Children's Services reports.

They didn't race to his house, but drove within the speed limits and didn't use any lights or siren. No need to get him or anyone else wound up. When Margie pulled to the curb near the house, Jones pulled up beside her.

"I'll go around back. Just in case. Don't stand in front of the door when you ring the bell."

Margie nodded. "Okay. Thanks. I'll give you a couple of minutes to get situated."

She watched Jones drive around the block, and used the interim to scope out the street. There was no car in front of Warner's house, and she couldn't see a garage in the back. But there might have been a gravel pad for parking; she couldn't be sure. Or the family might not even have two cars. Patty had to drive out to the park, and if Warner worked within the city or remotely, then he could bike or take the transit to work.

She didn't see anyone cross in front of the living room window while she was sitting there, but that didn't mean anything. They could all be in different parts of the house, Warner working on something for his job, washing the floor, or making other plans. He might have additional evidence to get rid of or a girlfriend that Patty hadn't known about.

Margie startled when her phone buzzed. She took a quick glance at it. Jones was ready in the back. She closed her eyes briefly to center herself, then got out of the car and walked up to the house. Standing to the side of the door, she rang and then pounded on the door with her fist loudly enough that anyone in the house would be able to hear. She didn't shout 'police.' That was mostly for cops on TV. She waited, listening for any sound from within or any movement in the window. Jones waited in back, quiet. No one trying to escape that way.

Everything was quiet. No sound of breaking glass. No footsteps within. Margie allowed herself a glance toward the street where she had expected a car to be parked. Where was he? Where would he go with the two little girls? It wasn't like he was taking them to the grandparents. He wouldn't want them anywhere near the Roscoes. She didn't know where his family was; he'd made no mention of them during their interview.

She rang and knocked a couple more times. Sometimes, residents were in the basement or the shower, somewhere they couldn't hear very well. Warner might have earphones on, listening to music as he cleaned. He could be gaming on his computer.

Eventually, Margie walked around back to where Jones was waiting. "Looks like he's out."

"Where do you think he is? Went out to get ice cream with the kids? Visiting family? Funeral home?"

Any of those were possibilities, but none of them rang true. Margie shook her head. She looked around the back yard. There was a gravel pad for parking, but no car. So, if they had two vehicles, Warner had taken the second out.

"We'll need a motor vehicles search to find out what he's driving."

Jones nodded. "Yeah. You going to put out an APB?"

"Yes... but I'd like to figure out where he's gone first. We should be able to figure this out."

"You don't think that he'd put the kids in danger, do you?"

"No. He doesn't have any reason to harm them."

Or did he? What if he did have another girlfriend and she didn't want kids? What if he'd never bonded with them in the first place and preferred to be on his own? What if the children were afraid of him and made him feel guilty whenever he looked at them?

There were plenty of reasons that he might want them out of the way. He might want a fresh start.

"I don't think so," she amended. "Warner didn't say anything that made me think he might..."

But the words sounded hollow in her own ears.

Where would he go?

If he didn't like the Roscoes, and of course he didn't, then he wouldn't take the children to them. And he hadn't taken them to the daycare.

He was not used to being home alone with them for more than an hour or two while he waited for Patty to get home from her job each day. He would quickly find out that single father-hood was no walk in the park.

Margie's brain caught on the phrase. *No walk in the park.*

She didn't think that he had taken them out for ice cream, but what about a walk in the park?

She walked back around the front of the house, Jones trailing her and asking something Margie didn't hear. She looked up and down the street. A neighborhood playground? No. He wouldn't need the car then. Somewhere farther away. In her memory, she saw Patty Roscoe's body in the water. She flashed on the children dipping minnows from the water from the little floating dock, their father standing back, watching them with unconcern.

They could fall into the water. Even though it wasn't deep and there was a lifesaver float right on the dock to be used if someone went into the water, something could still happen to them there.

And if a father's intentions were violent rather than just unconcerned that anything could happen to them...

There was a certain symmetry in the children drowning where their mother's body had been dumped—a way of giving them back to her.

"They've gone to the park," Margie told Jones. She was sure of it. She could feel it in her bones. "I'm going to head over there. We'll need a warrant for the house in case I'm wrong. Can you get that moving?"

"Yes, but I'm coming with you. You're not going on your own."

Margie nodded. "Yeah. Okay." She was probably right. That was just the kind of thing that a TV heroine would do—racing toward disaster, all by herself. No one to back her up.

"Do you know where it is? Have you been there before?" she asked Jones.

"Never been there before. But I studied the maps and the layout as part of the investigation. I can get out there."

"Okay. Just in case we get separated in traffic."

With a nod, the two of them separated to go back to their cars. Margie took one more look at the house for any sign that there was someone home, watching them through a window. But she didn't see any sign of life.

She checked through her GPS destinations and brought up the one for the park again. She knew where it was, but she didn't want to get it wrong. No wrong turns today.

CHAPTER SIXTEEN

*M*argie was impatient with the traffic lights on the way to the park, but she didn't want to use her lights and siren. They didn't know for sure that anyone's life was in danger. It was only a gut feeling that Warner was taking the children to the park. Even if they found him there, they couldn't assume that he had any intention to harm the children unless he took some action to indicate that he did. They would arrest him for his wife's murder, but that was all they could do to start with. MacDonald had said to bring him in for questioning. Hopefully, before they got very far, they would have confirmation that it was his voice on the recording and that the time record on the video put it in the window of time of Patty's death.

As she got out to the highway, she could see Jones's vehicle behind her. They were going to get there. They were going to arrest Scott Warner. They were going to take the children to their grandparents.

It would be a happy ending.

Not for Patty, but for everyone else. Her killer would be brought to justice. Her family would be reunited. They would be safe.

Margie couldn't see Warner at the creek where Patty's body had been dumped. She continued to drive around to the public parking lot but, rather than stopping, drove up over the sidewalk as close as she could to the education center, looking for Scott Warner's figure with the two little girls. She only had a vague picture of the little girls in mind, built from the blurry video of Arabella. Warner hadn't brought them with him the day he was interviewed. He hadn't shown her any family pictures. He hadn't wanted the police to have the opportunity to talk to the girls about what had happened to their mother.

Maybe he knew that Arabella knew something. Maybe he knew only that the girls knew their mother had come home, that they hadn't gone to bed waiting for her to return home.

She got out of her car, looking around. People were walking around, enjoying the mild weather—many of them stopping to look at the two vehicles driving up on the sidewalk. The cars were not marked squad cars, so people were probably pretty confused as to why the two women would drive their cars right up to the education center. Until they saw the women's vests and gun holsters. Then they'd have a pretty good idea.

Margie led the way around the education center, ignoring the queasiness and the pain in her chest as she climbed onto the walkways to go around the building. She could have told Jones to go around that side and gone around the other side of the education center on solid ground herself. But she hadn't been able to see Warner or the children in the playground on the other side of the education center. She had the little floating dock in her mind. That was where the children would be. That was what Scott Warner had in his mind. He would take them out there, show them how to dip their little nets into the water, and dump the contents into a bucket.

He would wait until they were happy and distracted. And then he would strike.

She could hardly breathe as she rushed along the walkway, up the stairs to the next level, and then out to the little bridge and pathway that would take them around the hill with the art installation and to the dock. Jones hurried behind her, asking questions that Margie couldn't hear or answer. It took everything she could to get over the grille on the bridge to where she felt safe.

CHAPTER SEVENTEEN

Warner was right where Margie had expected him to be. Standing on the floating dock with the two children kneeling in front of him, just like she had pictured. She had to blink her eyes a couple of times to clear them and make sure she wasn't really seeing the homeschooler dad or another small family group. Was she only seeing what she had thought she would see?

But Jones was swearing under her breath, hurrying along behind Margie.

"I'll fall back and flank him," Jones suggested. "You engage with him, talk to him, get him distracted. Keep him looking in your direction as much as possible. I'll get in behind him, closer to the children. We'll try to cut him off from them."

Margie nodded. Her brain objected that it wouldn't work, but she had to do what she could. Without a good plan of her own, she fell back on Detective Jones's.

"Mr. Warner," she called out, projecting her voice. She had a tough, no-nonsense, don't-mess-with-me cop voice. That, combined with a glare she had perfected as the mother of a teenager, was usually enough to get a suspect's attention and make him think twice about what he was doing.

He turned toward her, away from the two blond little girls with pails. Margie kept moving, walking on the path going past the dock, making him turn his body to keep facing her. His expression was one of shock. Eyes wide, skin pale, his mouth a slash of color that stood out in stark contrast to his skin.

"What are you doing here?" he demanded in an, aggrieved tone.

"We were looking for you. You weren't at your house, so I thought maybe you were here."

"What made you think I would be here?"

She didn't point out that since that was where his wife's body had been dumped, it seemed a logical choice. She didn't want to wind him up more, escalating the fear and anger he was already feeling. He felt vulnerable. He hadn't expected them to know that he was there. He had thought he would be safe and anonymous. He could bide his time until just the right moment, when no one would see or understand what he was doing. He had counted on being unknown and able to choose his timing.

"I'm glad we found you, Scott." She used a warm tone and his name. Make him feel seen. Make him feel validated. Important. "This has been a tough week on you."

"You're not kidding!" he agreed with a bark of laughter that was anything but amused.

"How are you feeling? Is there anything we can do for you?"

"*Why* are you here?" he asked again, shaking his head slightly.

"We just want to make sure that everyone is taken care of." She had planned to mention the girls, to ask him how they were doing, but she didn't want him to focus on the girls again. She wanted him to stay looking at her, talking to her, while Jones slipped between him and the children.

"You *know*." His tone was flat. Certain.

"What do we know?" Margie cocked her head as if she were curious. As if she didn't know what he was talking about.

"I had no idea. No way of knowing that she had given Arabella a phone." He shook his head in irritation, but did not turn to look back at his daughters. "I knew she was playing with one, but I thought it was Patty's old phone that didn't work anymore."

"What did she do with the phone?"

"Don't mess with me! I know that you know. The minute I saw that email go out to Patty's mother, I knew I was sunk."

Margie took a step closer to Warner, to keep his attention as much as to get close enough to do anything. Jones was staying quiet, trying to remain invisible and not to attract Warner's attention with her movements.

"How did you know about the email?" she asked Warner.

"I monitored Patty's email so that I would know if she was contacting her mother. Her friends. Trying to keep secrets from me. I would know if she was seeing someone behind my back."

Margie nodded slowly. "So you set something up so that you would be notified or copied any time she sent out an email."

"Of course I did. Anyone in my position would have done the same. I was protecting her. Protecting my family."

"Protecting them from what?"

"That mother of hers hated me. Right from the start, for no reason at all. How is that fair? How do you start off hating the person your daughter is dating without even knowing anything about them? Nothing at all!"

"That must have been hard for you."

"I was doing everything I could to keep us together. You don't know what it was like. How exhausting it was to keep on top of everything she was doing, to make sure that she was safe. That our family was safe from any outside forces. You have no idea how hard that is."

"No." Margie took another step toward him. They were almost close enough for her to grab him now. Just a few more steps, reaching out quickly, and she would have him. She didn't see a weapon, but that didn't mean he didn't have one. If he were doing everything he could to protect his family, then she wouldn't be at all surprised if he were carrying a knife or a gun. Or both. Gun violence was less common in Canada than it was in the States, but it wasn't nonexistent. People still shot each other. With registered or unregistered weapons. Warner didn't have a firearms license, but that didn't mean he hadn't acquired a gun somewhere.

"What happened? What was it that drove a wedge between the two of you?" she asked with as much compassion as she could muster. "Was it just her mother? Or were there other things? Money? Other pressures?"

"Her mother was a thorn in my side. She said that she wouldn't have anything to do with Patty while the two of us were together, and it was tearing Patty up. I thought that as the girls got older, it wouldn't be as much of an issue. She would establish a mother-daughter relationship with them, and her connection to her mother wouldn't matter so much. But I think the opposite was true. The older the girls got, the more she wanted to make up with her mother. I told her she couldn't. She couldn't be the one to give in first. And the only thing her mother would be happy with was the two of us getting divorced." He gave Margie a fierce look. "And we weren't getting a divorce."

Not for anything. He would kill her first.

Margie cast around for something else to ask him. But at that moment, he realized that Jones was there, working her way between them, cutting the children off from Warner.

Making a noise like an enraged bull, he threw himself at Jones. She wasn't expecting it, but she was well-trained and solidly built, and she absorbed the initial impact.

"Mr. Warner, you are under arrest for assaulting an officer of the law," she told him in a calm, clear voice, grasping his arm.

But somehow, he slipped out of her grasp. Having failed in pushing her farther away from his family, he tried the reverse. Before Margie could take one step forward to stop him, he had rushed at the girls, sweeping them out into the water. There were a couple of strangled screams of surprise and fear before they went under the surface of the dark water. Margie ran toward them, her mind a horrified blank, unable to process what had happened or what she should do about it. Warner charged her, bowling her over. The collision knocked the wind out of her, and she was left on the ground, her head spinning. She stared up at one of the towering monoliths, then forced herself to move. Roll over. Regain her feet and her balance, look around for Warner. But the babies were behind her, and what was she going to do about them?

"Go!" Jones shouted at her. "I've got the kids. Go after him!"

Margie's movements were slow, like swimming through concrete. She saw Jones pick up the lifesaver and toss it into the water. As she turned away to look for Warner, she heard a splash and knew that Jones had jumped in.

CHAPTER EIGHTEEN

*W*arner was on the run. Margie shut everything else out and focused on gaining on him. He couldn't be allowed to get back to his car and make an escape. He had killed his wife, had intended to kill his children, and she was not going to let him get away. She didn't know if he had planned to kill himself too, but running suggested to her that his instinct to preserve his own life and liberty was still strong.

Her feet crunched through the gravel of the pathway. Warner was headed for the education center, toward the big pool and the walkways elevated over the water. Margie's mind rebelled against the idea of running toward them. The last thing she wanted was to end up plummeting into the water. But she had a job to do. She was a cop and she couldn't let her phobia control her decisions. She had been told more than once that the only way to overcome her fear was by exposing herself to it. So in reality, running toward the water at a breakneck pace was good for her.

She had a stitch in her side. She had let her running habit fall by the wayside when she had moved to Calgary. If she wanted to stay in shape, she would have to get up earlier in the morning to run, and morning was not her best time. But she was getting out of shape, and should at least consider it.

Warner entered the walkways. He slowed down, but was still moving at a pretty quick clip. Margie put on a burst of speed to catch up with him and stepped onto the walkway herself. Her heart was in her throat. She could barely breathe. Her vision was narrow so that she could only see what was in front of her. She knew the way out. She needed to keep pushing forward, and then she would, in a couple of minutes, be on solid ground again. She could tackle Warner in the parking lot. Cuff him and take him into custody. It would all work out just fine.

She was no longer running, but was pushing herself to move as quickly as she could. The walkway felt narrow and unsteady. She knew she was suspended above the water, and her brain was telling her that at any minute, she could die. She went up the stairs to the second. She listened, but could no longer hear Warner's footsteps clanging ahead of her. He must already be off of the walkways and into the parking lot. That meant that she didn't have much farther to go.

A blow hit her from the side as she turned a corner. She was stunned and thrown off balance. Where had it come from? She grabbed onto the rail to steady herself and to try to reorient herself. She could see the water below her. Just her and a thin grille topped with a railing to keep her separated from it. Whose idea had it been to put young children and the frail and infirm so close to danger? Why had they thought it such a good idea to build out on the water instead of on solid, safe land?

She caught a flash of his face in front of her—an angry, maniacal grimace. "Leave me alone! You think a woman is going to get the better of me? Never!"

Before she had a chance to anticipate what he was going to do, he slammed into her again, the weight of his body throwing her against the low barrier. His hands grasped her elbow and knee, and he lifted her off of the ground. Using their momentum, he had her up and over the railing before she could catch hold of anything.

She was airborne, arms and legs flailing frantically for something to stop her fall. Then she was in the water. It drove all of the air out of her lungs when she hit the surface and then sank beneath it. Shockingly cold. The water enveloped her. She couldn't see. She held her breath and flailed and hit bottom. She was disoriented, feeling the mucky, slimy floor of the pond bottom beneath her. Had her brain blocked out the sensation of falling through the water? It seemed as if the journey to the bottom of the pond had taken only an instant.

She tried to push herself up, her hands sinking into the mud and not propelling her toward the surface. She tried to swim up toward the surface, and her hands broke out of the water.

Margie repositioned herself feet downward, and tried to stand. The muck prevented her from doing it very gracefully, sucking her feet and ankles down, but the water was not even to her waist. Margie took in gasps of air and tried to settle her panicked body and brain. She could breathe. She wasn't drowning. But she was in the middle of the pond, sinking almost to her knees in muck.

She looked around, trying to figure out the best way to get out. The education center towered above her, and the walls were sheer rock, too steep to climb.

Someone was yelling at her. Margie blinked foul water from her eyes and tried to focus on the voice.

"…okay?" she heard from somewhere up above her. Margie tipped back her head to look at the figure standing on the edge. Finkle, his hands making anxious movements.

"I'm okay," she confirmed, still gasping.

"Can you turn around? Or are you stuck?"

Margie lifted her feet one at a time, pulling them out of the sucking mud and looking for somewhere more solid to put them down. The water was frigid. She was already shivering.

"Over to your left, you see the rock steps going down into the water?"

Margie saw a stonework of long, shallow steps. A couple of other workers stood there gaping at her.

"Just make your way over there," Finkle told her in a calm, even voice.

Margie waded through the mud, one painstaking step at a time. It would undoubtedly be faster to lie down on the surface of the water and swim across, unimpeded by the mud, except that she had never learned to swim. Even floating was an issue for Margie, especially with her face in or close to the surface of the water. When she finally got close enough to the steps, Finkle was waiting there, still encouraging her in a measured, reassuring voice. Finkle reached out a hand for her. His grip was strong. With his help, she was able to drag her feet one last time out of the mud and crawl back onto solid ground. It was an effort to break the surface tension. And then she was above the water.

Finkle patted her on the shoulder. "You're good. Keep going."

At the top, back on firm ground, someone wrapped a blanket around her.

"Ambulance is on the way. Just sit down here and stay warm."

Margie shook her head. She felt better standing. Like she was a grown-up, not a little kid. She wiped foul pond water from her face, looking around. Jones was a short distance away, mothering the two children, all three of them soaked. But they seemed to be in better shape than Margie, who was shaking like a leaf and having problems catching her breath.

"Are you okay?" Jones asked, looking over at her.

Margie cleared her throat. "I wasn't planning on going into the water."

"No," Jones gave a little laugh. "None of that was planned."

"Where did he go?" Margie looked at Finkle. "Did you see where Warner went? What direction…?"

"Back into the city. Headed north. Couldn't tell you more than that."

"They've got hawks out," Jones said.

Margie didn't understand at first. Jones pointed to a black helicopter in the sky some distance away. Helicopter Air Watch for Community Safety—HAWCS. The police services helicopter.

"Does that mean they know where he is?"

"I don't know. Need to get back to the radio in my car to touch base. I don't think either of our phones are going to work. They called 9-1-1," Jones motioned to the various education center workers who were standing around, some helping and some just watching. "And the chopper was scrambled pretty quickly. I called in the APB on Warner's vehicles as we were driving over, so they knew what he was driving. But they'll be waiting for an update from us."

"We'd better do that, then." Margie attempted to squeeze some of the water out of her clothes and headed to the cars. At least they weren't very far away. Jones left the children under the supervision of one of the teachers and followed.

They stood outside of the vehicles, dripping everywhere, while Jones called on her radio, asking to be put in contact with the homicide department and with the HAWCS and other police on the ground. In a few minutes, they were all on the same channel, exchanging what information they could.

Margie bent her head close to listen. "He's in Erin Woods? I know where that is. That's not far from my place."

"You want to go over?" Jones asked. "I'm not sure how close we'll be able to get to the action, but you're going to have to go home to get changed anyway."

Margie nodded. "Yeah. Let's do it."

"More than likely, they'll just tell us to stay out of the way. But you can at least see HAWCS up close."

"Yes."

"You know your way around there? How to get there? Do you want to meet up in a particular place if we get separated?"

"I don't know my way at all." Margie reached into her car to grab her GPS. She tapped in Erin Woods and waited for something to come up on the screen. "Uh… the Community Center. How about that? We'll meet there, or get as close to it as we can."

CHAPTER NINETEEN

here were squad cars everywhere. The big armored rescue vehicle used by the CPS Tactical Unit was stopped in the middle of the Community Center parking lot. Both still dripping, Jones and Margie were directed to the tactical unit leader who got what details he could from them as to what had happened at Ralph Klein Park.

"So, what is your evaluation of his state of mind?" Sergeant Burns queried. "He's on the run, so you would think he was concerned with self-preservation, but if we've got a man who might be armed and who really doesn't have any reason to live, we need to know that before going in."

"Do you know where he is?" Margie asked, trying to discern from the activity around her just what the status of the pursuit was.

"He ditched his vehicle and took off on foot, so he can't have gotten far." HAWCS continued to buzz around overhead, looking for him. "We'll have scent dogs in a few minutes and they'll find him. But how he's going to behave once he's cornered, that's always a concern."

"He killed his wife. We have the proof and he knows it. He knows he's going down for it. He's looking at years of incarceration. He went to the park to drown his children. What I don't know is whether he planned to kill himself, or to disappear and start a new life somewhere else."

"So he doesn't have anything to lose when we catch up to him. Death or prison. Those are his only options."

Margie nodded. She looked at the armored Tactical Unit members. "Be careful. I don't think he's armed, but there's no way to know for sure. I don't think he's going to come easy."

Sergeant Burns nodded briefly. He'd probably already guessed that, but it was vital for him to have as much information as he could get.

"Is there any way we can help?" Margie asked.

"You don't have a relationship with this guy?"

"I've interviewed him before. He wasn't antagonistic then. But today..." She looked down at her dripping uniform. "I don't know whether he intended for me to drown, but he did throw me over a railing into the water."

"So, no," Burns said dryly. He looked at Detective Jones. "And you?" He observed her soaked uniform as well.

"No. Although I can tell him that his kids are okay. If he thinks he succeeded in drowning them, he might be more desperate. If he knows they're okay..."

Burns scribbled notes into a notepad. "Whoever tracks him down can pass that along. You're right; it might be just enough to make the difference between him being taken into custody quietly and suicide by cop."

He didn't tell them anything else they could do, so Jones and Margie stood around awkwardly, watching the rest of the officers who were involved moving from one position to another and reporting to Burns. The dog handler arrived with a German shepherd at his side and, after a few minutes, the dog was put onto the scent he was to track. Margie watched him put nose to ground and cast around. She imagined Stella trying to do the same thing. Stella sometimes thought she was a hunting dog, but she wasn't very good at it. She could track a quarry a few feet, but then she lost the scent. The shepherd with the dog handler seemed to be up to the job. In a couple of minutes, he was pulling hard on the harness, following Warner's trail from the car he had ditched. He led his handler to the far corner of the school field, which then joined with a pathway, out of their sight. Margie looked at Jones, then around at the houses close to the Community Center. There were a lot of residents looking out their windows or doors or hanging around the sidewalk. They looked up at HAWCS and took pictures of the tactical vehicle with their phones.

"The Twitterverse is buzzing," Jones observed. "Let's just hope that Warner isn't following it."

Wherever Warner was, crouched between houses or hiding under someone's car, Margie didn't imagine he was tapping on his phone, checking out all of the social media.

Would he hide? Would he try to walk out of the area? Get on a bus and escape the police net? She really wanted this guy. She wanted to make sure he was put behind bars for as long as possible.

She tried to squeeze more water out of her chilly, chafing clothes.

"You should go home and change," Jones suggested.

"I know. But I want to see how this all ends up. It won't take long, right? Just a few minutes?"

"You never know. Sometimes a standoff can go on for hours before the person finally gives up to the police."

"I'm going to stay for a while, at least. I really want to see them catch this guy."

CHAPTER TWENTY

They heard the dog barking in the distance. They all stood as still as statues, waiting for gunshots and explosions. Margie could hear Sergeant Burns's radio crackling, the reports coming in one on top of the other. He had been spotted entering the back yard of a house across from Erin Woods Park. The Tactical Unit worked to surround and contain him. Still no shots fired. Margie breathed shallowly, not wanting to miss anything. Over the radio, she heard the shouted command for him to come out with his hands up. Warner yelled back, wanting to know the status of his children and of the police women at the park.

Margie and Jones listened to the information being relayed back to him. Would their reassurances be enough to deescalate him? Was he past that, too desperate to be calmed down?

No shots.

He exchanged words with them another time. And another. Margie started to breathe normally again. He was having a conversation. He had not attacked or made threats. He hadn't said he had a weapon and charged one of the team.

It was working. They could all breathe again. Margie would be filling in paperwork for days, but they would have him. The children were safe. The other people in Warner's life that might have crossed him one too many times were safe.

Eventually, a voice came over Burns's radio.

"We're clear. Suspect in custody."

❧

MARGIE FOUND she didn't care about the paperwork. She was happy to go home to change and then drive back downtown with towels on her car seat and report back to the office to be debriefed and get started on the pile of reports that would need to be filed.

"The Roscoes have the children," Cruz told Margie. "They were taken straight there. Children's Services will follow up to evaluate the home and finalize the placement, but they will be safe with family tonight, not in foster care."

"But they don't know the Roscoes. So it's still going to feel strange and foreign to them."

"Better to be with family, though. They can start settling in and getting healed, instead of being disrupted with a series of placements and maybe getting separated. And I suspect they know Grandma and Grandpa better than we think."

Margie raised her brows. "Oh? I didn't think Mrs. Roscoe was lying when she said she hadn't had any contact with them."

Cruz pointed to Margie's computer screen, where the video Mrs. Roscoe had received from her daughter's email account was still frozen in a small square in the corner of the desktop. Margie pressed the 'play' triangle, and it started from the beginning, Arabella talking herself through the instructions that her mother had given her. Tapping on the picture of Grandma.

Cruz nodded. "She knows who Grandma is. Her mother showed her pictures and talked to her at least enough to recognize the picture and know who it was. Maybe they didn't have any direct contact, but the little girl had been told who she was, and that was who she was supposed to send the recording too. She knew that Grandma would do something to help them when she received the video."

CHAPTER TWENTY-ONE

*I*n a few days, Margie was with her own grandparent, secure in the knowledge that Warner was behind bars awaiting trial and Patty's daughters were safe. Moushoom had been quick to agree to go with them to Glenbow Ranch Provincial Park for a golf cart tour, and after that, to MacKay's for ice cream.

"You are in for a treat," he told them, eyes shining. "MacKay's is a tradition."

And traditions were important in Margie's family and community.

"I didn't think you'd know about them," she told him, glancing at him in surprise as she navigated the highway between the Park and Cochrane. Ice cream was just two kilometers away.

"I took your mother there when she was a little girl," Moushoom said. "We were just visiting then, I hadn't moved to Calgary yet, but MacKay's was there back then, and it was one of our favorite outings."

Margie's mother had always loved ice cream. Margie looked at Christina and grinned. It was a family trait.

Jones had told Margie that MacKay's had dozens of flavors, but she had still not expected the densely-written chalkboard she saw when she got there. She and Christina stared at it with their mouths open, marveling at all of the options.

"Bubblegum," Christina pointed out almost immediately.

Margie remembered blue stains on many of Christina's collars when she was a little girl, when blue bubble-gum ice cream had been her favorite treat. So sticky and messy. At least now, as a teenager, Margie wouldn't have to worry about Christina staining all of her clothes.

"What is 'barn door'?" Margie asked no one in particular.

A helpful patron described the ice cream concoction that included marshmallows, chocolate chips, chocolate chunks, Reese's peanut butter cups, fudge brownie bits, cookie dough, nuts, Oreo cookie crumbs, and coconut.

"Oh, my."

It wasn't going to be an easy choice. They had the cherry custard and cotton candy, two flavors she had enjoyed as a child when camping by the lake.

"Maple bacon," Christina murmured reverently.

"I thought you were vegetarian now."

Christina opened her mouth, considering. "I don't think maple bacon ice cream counts," she said finally, without bothering to give an argument as to why that was.

"I know what I am having," Moushoom announced.

Margie looked at him. She was expecting to have to read the board to him. But either his eyes or his memory was better than she had expected.

"What are you having, Moushoom?"

"Nanaimo bar."

"Oh…" That was tempting. But if Moushoom was getting it, then she was sure he would allow her to taste a bit of his custard and chocolate concoction. Sharing ice cream during a pandemic might not be such a good idea. She'd get a spoon and have a taste before he started it. That way, neither was contaminating the other.

They were getting to the front of the line, and Margie still hadn't made up her mind. She skimmed over the board once more.

"What is 'shark attack'?"

"Blue raspberry ice cream with red raspberry jam ripples," the young woman at the counter advised. She didn't have to check. She probably told ten people an hour all day long. Behind her face shield, forehead and temples glistened with sweat despite working with frozen desserts all day.

Margie's mind went back to Warner attacking her at the park and throwing her into the water, thinking she wouldn't make it out alive.

No, it wouldn't be shark attack. Not this time.

RALPH KLEIN PARK

The Ralph Klein Park is much smaller than the previous two parks in the series, but this little place packs a punch with manmade wetland features, public art installations, a community orchard of apple and pear trees, a unique playground with a zip line, and an education center.

Ralph Klein Park is on the east side of Calgary, and like Glenbow Ranch Provincial Park, opened in 2011.

It is named after former Calgary mayor and Alberta premier Ralph Klein, who lived to witness its opening and passed away in 2013.

Did you enjoy this book? Reviews and recommendations are vital to making a book successful.

Please leave a review at your favorite book store or review site and share it with your friends.

Don't miss the following bonus material:
Sign up for mailing list to get a free ebook
Read a sneak preview chapter
Other books by P.D. Workman
Learn more about the author

Sign up for my mailing list at pdworkman.com and get Gluten-Free Murder for free!

PREVIEW OF SHE WORE MOURNING

ZACHARY GOLDMAN MYSTERIES #1

———

More Parks Pat Mysteries are planned.
While you are waiting for them, why not check out
Zachary Goldman Mysteries?

CHAPTER 1

ZACHARY GOLDMAN STARED DOWN the telephoto lens at the subjects before him. It was one of those days that left tourists gaping over the gorgeous scenery. Dark trees against crisp white snow, with the mountains as a backdrop. Like the picture on a Christmas card.

The thought made Zachary feel sick.

But he wasn't looking at the scenery. He was looking at the man and the woman in a passionate embrace. The pretty young woman's cheeks were flushed pink, more likely with her excitement than the cold, since she had barely stepped out of her car to greet the man. He had a swarthier complexion and a thin black beard, and was currently turned away from Zachary's camera.

Zachary wasn't much to look at himself. Average height, black hair cut too short, his own three-day growth of beard not hiding how pinched and pale his face was. He'd never considered himself a good catch.

He waited patiently for them to move, to look around at their surroundings so that he could get a good picture of their faces.

They thought they were alone; that no one could see them without being seen. They hadn't counted on the fact that Zachary had been surveilling them for a couple of weeks and had known where they would go. They gave him lots of warning so that he could park his car out of sight, camouflage himself in the trees, and settle in to wait for their appearance. He was no amateur; he'd been a private investigator since she had been choosing wedding dresses for her Barbie dolls.

He held down the shutter button to take a series of shots as they came up for air and looked around at the magnificent surroundings, smiling at each other, eyes shining.

All the while, he was trying to keep the negative thoughts at bay. Why had he fallen into private detection? It was one of the few ways he could make a living using his skill with a camera. He could have chosen another profession. He didn't need to spend his whole life following other people, taking pictures of their most private moments. What was the real point of his job? He destroyed lives, something he'd had his fill of long ago. When was the last time he'd brought a smile to a client's face? A real, genuine smile? He had wanted to make a difference in people's lives; to exonerate the innocent.

Zachary's phone started to buzz in his pocket. He lowered the camera and turned around, walking farther into the grove of trees. He had the pictures he needed. Anything else would be overkill.

He pulled out his phone and looked at it. Not recognizing the number, he swiped the screen to answer the call.

"Goldman Investigations."

"Uh... yes... Is this Mr. Goldman?" a voice inquired. Older, female, with a tentative quaver.

"Yes, this is Zachary," he confirmed, subtly nudging her away from the 'mister.'

"Mr. Goldman, my name is Molly Hildebrandt."

He hoped she wasn't calling her about her sixty-something-year-old husband and his renewed interest in sex. If it was another infidelity case, he was going to have to turn it down for his own sanity. He would even take a lost dog or wedding ring. As long as the ring wasn't on someone else's finger now.

"Mrs. Hildebrandt. How can Goldman Investigations help you?"

Of course, she had probably already guessed that Goldman Investigations consisted of only one employee. Most people seemed to sense that from the size of his advertisements. From the fact that he listed a post office box number instead of a business suite downtown or in one of the newer commercial areas. It wasn't really a secret.

"I don't know whether you have been following the news at all about Declan Bond, the little boy who drowned…?"

Zachary frowned. He trudged back toward his car.

"I'm familiar with the basics," he hedged. A four- or five-year-old boy whose round face and feathery dark hair had been pasted all over the news after a search for a missing child had ended tragically.

"They announced a few weeks ago that it was determined to be an accident."

Zachary ground his teeth. "Yes…?"

"Mr. Goldman, I was Declan's grandma." Her voice cracked. Zachary waited, listening to her sniffles and sobs as she tried to get herself under control. "I'm sorry. This has been very difficult for me. For everyone."

"Yes."

"Mr. Goldman, I don't believe that it was an accident. I'm looking for someone who would investigate the matter privately."

Zachary breathed out. A homicide investigation? Of a child? He'd told himself that he would take anything that wasn't infidelity, but if there was one thing that was more depressing than couples cheating on each other, it was the death of a child.

"I'm sure there are private investigators that would be more qualified for a homicide case than I am, Mrs. Hildebrandt. My schedule is pretty full right now."

Which, of course, was a lie. He had the usual infidelities, insurance investigations, liabilities, and odd requests. The dregs of the private investigation business. Nothing substantial like a homicide. It was a high-profile case. A lot of volunteers had shown up to help, expecting to find a child who had wandered out of his own yard, expecting to find him dirty and crying, not floating face down in a pond. A lot of people had mourned the death of a child they hadn't even known existed before his disappearance.

"I need your help, Mr. Goldman. Zachary. I can't afford a big name, but you've got good references. You've investigated deaths before. Can't you help me?"

He wondered who she had talked to. It wasn't like there were a lot of people who would give him a bad reference. He was competent and usually got the job done, but he wasn't a big name.

"I could meet with you," he finally conceded. "The first consultation is free. We'll see what kind of a case you have and whether I want to take it. I'm not making any promises at this point. Like I said, my schedule is pretty full already."

She gave a little half-sob. "Thank you. When are you able to come?"

———

After he had hung up, Zachary climbed into his car, putting his camera down on the floor in front of the passenger seat where it couldn't fall, and started the car. For a while, he sat there, staring out the front windshield at the magical, sparkling, Christmas-card scene. Every year, he told himself it would be better. He would get over it and be able to move on and to enjoy the holiday season like everyone else. Who cared about his crappy childhood experiences? People moved on.

And when he had married Bridget, he had thought he was going to achieve it. They would have a fairy-tale Christmas. They would have hot chocolate after skating at the public rink. They would wander down Main Street looking at the lights and the crèche in front of the church. They would open special, meaningful presents from each other.

But they'd fought over Christmas. Maybe it was Zachary's

fault. Maybe he had sabotaged it with his gloom. The season brought with it so much baggage. There had been no skating rink. No hot chocolate, only hot tempers. No walks looking at the lights or the nativity. They had practically thrown their gifts at each other, flouncing off to their respective corners to lick their wounds and pout away the holiday.

He'd still cherished the thought that perhaps the next year there would be a baby. What could be more perfect than Christmas with a baby? It would unite them. Make them a real family. Just like Zachary had longed for since he'd lost his own family. He and Bridget and a baby. Maybe even twins. Their own little family in their own little happy bubble.

But despite a positive pregnancy test, things had gone horribly wrong.

Zachary stared at the bright white scenery and blinked hard, trying to shake off the shadows of the past. The past was past. Over and done. This year he was back to baching it for Christmas. Just him and a beer and *It's a Wonderful Life* on TV.

He put the car in reverse and didn't look into the rear-view mirror as he backed up, even knowing about the precipice behind him. He'd deliberately parked where he'd have to back up toward the cliff when he was done. There was a guardrail, but if he backed up too quickly, the car would go right through it, and who could say whether it had been accidental or deliberate? He had been cold-stone sober and had been out on a job. Mrs. Hildebrandt could testify that he had been calm and sober during their call. It would be ruled an accident.

But his bumper didn't even touch the guardrail before he shifted into drive and pulled forward onto the road.

He'd meet with the grandmother. Then, assuming he did not take the case, there would always be another opportunity.

Life was full of opportunities.

———

She Wore Mourning, book #1 of the *Zachary Goldman Mysteries* series is available now at pdworkman.com

ABOUT THE AUTHOR

Award-winning and USA Today bestselling author P.D. (Pamela) Workman writes riveting mystery/suspense and young adult books dealing with mental illness, addiction, abuse, and other real-life issues. For as long as she can remember, the blank page has held an incredible allure and from a very young age she was trying to write her own books.

Workman wrote her first complete novel at the age of twelve and continued to write as a hobby for many years. She started publishing in 2013. She has won several literary awards from Library Services for Youth in Custody for her young adult fiction. She currently has over 60 published titles and can be found at pdworkman.com.

Born and raised in Alberta, Workman has been married for over 25 years and has one son.

❧

Please visit P.D. Workman at pdworkman.com to see what else she is working on, to join her mailing list, and to link to her social networks.

❧

If you enjoyed this book, please take the time to recommend it to other purchasers with a review or star rating and share it with your friends!

facebook.com/pdworkmanauthor

twitter.com/pdworkmanauthor

instagram.com/pdworkmanauthor

amazon.com/author/pdworkman

bookbub.com/authors/p-d-workman

goodreads.com/pdworkman

linkedin.com/in/pdworkman

pinterest.com/pdworkmanauthor

youtube.com/pdworkman